AF241568

PIES & PLANS

BOOK 5 IN THE PAWS & PASTRIES SERIES

BARBARA HINSKE

CASA DEL NORTHERN PUBLISHING

ALSO BY BARBARA HINSKE

Available at Amazon in Print, Audio, and for Kindle

The Rosemont Series

Coming to Rosemont

Weaving the Strands

Uncovering Secrets

Drawing Close

Bringing Them Home

Shelving Doubts

Restoring What Was Lost

No Matter How Far

When Dreams There Be

Waves of Grace

Threads of Kindness

Love and Legacy

Novellas

The Night Train

The Christmas Club (adapted

for The Hallmark Channel, 2019)

Paws & Pastries

Sweets & Treats

Snowflakes, Cupcakes & Kittens

Tarts & Turnovers

Pies & Plans

Workout Wishes & Valentine Kisses

Wishes of Home

Wishful Tails

Back in the Pack

Novels in the Guiding Emily Series

Guiding Emily (adapted for The Hallmark Channel, 2023)

The Unexpected Path

Over Every Hurdle

Down the Aisle

From the Heart

Growing the Circle

Novels in the "Who's There?!" Collection

Deadly Parcel

Final Circuit

CONNECT WITH BARBARA HINSKE

Sign up for her newsletter at **BarbaraHinske.com**
  Goodreads.com/BarbaraHinske
  Facebook.com/BHinske
  Instagram/barbarahinskeauthor
  Pinterest.com/BarbaraHinske
  BookBub/Barbara Hinske
  Twitter(X)/Barbara Hinske
  TikTok.com/BarbaraHinske
  Search for **Barbara Hinske on YouTube**
  bhinske@gmail.com

PIES & PLANS

This book may not be reproduced in whole or in part without written permission of the author, with the exception of brief quotations within book reviews or articles. This book is a work of fiction. Any resemblance to actual persons, living or dead, or places or events is coincidental.

Copyright © 2025 Barbara Hinske.

Cover by Elizabeth Mackey, Copyright © 2025

All rights reserved.

ISBN: 9781969752117

Library of Congress Control Number: 2025927987

Casa del Northern Publishing

Phoenix, Arizona

No AI Training: Without in any way limiting the author's exclusive rights under copyright, any use of this publication to "train" generative artificial intelligence (AI) technologies to generate text is expressly prohibited. The author reserves all rights to license uses of this work for generative AI training and development of machine learning language models.

To my remarkable mother and grandmother, who instilled in me a passion for baking and—most importantly—modeled how to build a loving home .

Clara Conway released her hair from the tight bun at the nape of her neck and allowed her long, chestnut-colored locks to curl around her shoulders. She swiped tinted lip gloss across her lips and glanced at her reflection in the mirror. She looked like a woman about to collapse from exhaustion, not one about to tour a potential wedding venue with her fiancé.

She'd risen at 2:30 that morning and unlocked the back door to Sweets & Treats at 3:00 a.m. It was now 1:00 in the afternoon, and she'd been on her feet the entire time.

Owning and operating her own patisserie had been her lifelong dream—but sometimes that dream felt more like a nightmare. Two of her bakers had called in sick to care for their children. The beginning of the school year always saw high absenteeism. Her crew often joked that elementary school classrooms were like Petri dishes.

Clara didn't mind, of course. Parents needed to care for their children, and she was happy to step in to help. Still, she was bone-tired.

She rummaged through her purse until she found the small, round container of concealer. Popping open the lid, she dabbed the creamy makeup under her eyes, doing her best to blend the edges. When she stepped back, the face staring at her looked like a raccoon.

"Great," she muttered. "I've made it worse." Tearing a paper towel from the dispenser, she scrubbed away the too-bright concealer.

Her phone buzzed in her purse. That would be her fiancé, Kurt Holbrook, letting her know he was in the rear parking lot to pick her up for the forty-five-minute drive to the venue. He was never early, but she knew he was eager to begin their wedding plans. Clara slung her purse over her shoulder and walked from the workroom into the storefront.

Maisie Johanson stood behind the cash register. She handed a pink bakery box and a signed credit card receipt to a customer. "Thank you so much for your business!"

The woman exclaimed, "I am *so* looking forward to eating these cupcakes! My neighbor told me you're the best bakery in the state."

"We like to think so," Maisie said with a grin as the customer left the shop.

"Kurt just texted," Clara said. "He's out back waiting for me. Thank you so much for coming in on short notice to help, Maisie."

"Anytime," Maisie said warmly. "You know I love this place—and how much I miss it. I can't work full-time anymore, but I'm always happy to help when you're in a tight spot. You'd better get going," Maisie added, waving her toward the back. "Take as much time as you need, and don't worry about a thing here. I'll stay and close up."

"You're a lifesaver," Clara said, smiling at her elderly friend and business partner as she turned toward the workroom.

"Let's talk soon. I can't wait to hear how the wedding plans are shaping up!" Maisie called after her, her voice full of affection for the young woman she loved like a daughter.

Clara pushed through the back door of the patisserie —but Kurt's SUV was nowhere in sight. Maybe he'd decided to pick her up out front. She pulled her phone from her purse and opened his message.

Can't make our appointment. Had to step in at the last minute to cover an emergency hearing. I'm so sorry. If you want, go without me. If not, I'll reschedule. Please let me know either way.

Clara let her purse slip from her shoulder and onto the asphalt. Leaning against the brick wall, she exhaled slowly. The last thing she wanted to do was drive forty-five minutes each way when she could barely keep her eyes open. Her shoulders relaxed in relief.

She typed quickly:

No worries. I want to wait for you to be there. I'm short-handed again today, so it's just as well. Call me later, and we'll regroup.

She tapped send and listened for the soft whoosh that confirmed her message had gone through.

The early autumn air held the faintest chill. The brick wall against her back was warm from the sun. Clara closed her eyes, tipped her face upward, and inhaled deeply. It felt heavenly to be still, doing absolutely nothing.

The squeal of the rear door's rusty hinges jolted her from her reverie. Joan, her workroom supervisor, stepped outside. She stopped short when she spotted Clara.

"I thought you and Kurt were on your way to visit that potential wedding venue," Joan said, as she carried two bags of trash to the dumpster.

Clara ran a hand through her hair, wondering how long she'd been standing there. Had she fallen asleep on her feet? A quick glance at her watch made her cringe—fifteen minutes had passed. "That was the plan," she said lightly. "But he must have gotten held up. I'm sure he'll text me soon."

She felt a flicker of guilt for the white lie. Kurt hadn't left her in the lurch—she just didn't want to admit she'd nodded off standing up. Joan had already scolded her for overworking. "Let's go inside and review our plans for tomorrow," Clara said, pushing herself off the wall.

Joan nodded. "We've had a good day, but things have slowed down."

"Shall we send Maisie home?"

"I already told her to head out," Joan said. "I heard her call Josef—he's on his way to pick her up."

"Thank you," Clara said. "I know you've been putting in extra hours, too. It's almost closing time. We'll soon be able to flip the sign to Closed and walk out the back door to our cars."

"I'm not gonna lie," Joan said with a tired grin. "I like the sound of that."

CHAPTER 2

Clara pulled the plaid woolen throw up to her chin and snuggled closer to Kurt. Noelle, her faithful terrier mix, jumped onto the loveseat beside them and settled against Clara's leg.

"Is it getting too cold?" he asked, turning toward her and planting a kiss on the top of her head. "Do you want to go inside?"

The flames in the fire pit danced against the night sky.

"Not yet," she replied. "It's so cozy out here, cuddled up by the fire. It'll be too cold to sit outside soon. We'll be cooped up inside for the winter before long. I want to savor this while we can."

"You're right," he said. "Although I wouldn't mind being snowed in with you for a few days."

"That sounds appealing." She smiled. "I'm looking

forward to being married and spending every night with you." She glanced at him. "Did the wedding venue get back to you with a new date for us to take a tour?"

"I'm glad you reminded me," Kurt said. "I've got a three-week trial coming up, so our next opportunity to meet with them is in four weeks."

"Geez," Clara said. "This wedding is taking forever to plan."

"Because neither of us has time to plan it," he replied, raking his hand through his thick dark hair. "Maybe we should hire a wedding planner. What do you think?"

"Probably," she said. "I only have a handful of guests to invite, but you've lived here your whole life and you're a prominent member of the legal community. I understand why your guest list tops two hundred."

"I never wanted a big wedding," Kurt said. "But once I started jotting down names, I realized I couldn't invite some people and not others without hurting feelings. It's a small town—those details matter."

"I get it," she said, stifling a yawn. "I sometimes wish we could just wake up married."

"Isn't there anyone you really want at the wedding?"

Clara tucked her feet under her and leaned back to look at him. "Of course there is. Maisie and Josef have to be there. And of course I want Joan from the bakery— and Laura, Ian, and Tabitha. The Trents might be my landlords, but they've become like family to me."

Kurt stared into the flames. The only sound was the soft crackling of the logs. "Let's do it," he said finally.

"Do what?"

"Get married. Now." He faced her.

"You mean elope?" she asked. "I don't want to elope —Maisie and Josef would be heartbroken."

"I don't want to elope either," he said. "But we don't need a big, fancy wedding. Neither of us has time to plan it—and, honestly, I don't think either of us really wants that."

"What about your two hundred guests?"

"Let's throw a big party for them after we're married."

"Oh, I love that idea!" Clara hopped onto her knees, eyes shining. "We could hold it at Bloom Cottage in the spring. We'll have brunch and games for the kids. Maybe even an egg hunt!"

Kurt chuckled. "The idea really appeals to you, doesn't it?"

"It certainly does," Clara said. "Let's get married at Bloom Cottage, too. If the weather's nice, we'll be on the porch. If not, we'll tie the knot in front of the stone fireplace in the living room."

"My grandparents, may they rest in peace, would be thrilled that I'm getting married at their old homestead. We could invite the people you just mentioned, plus my secretary—she's been with me since I was a newly minted lawyer—and Brad. I consider him more than just the man who manages my rental properties. I was going to ask him to be my best man."

"Counting us, that would be ten people—eleven, including the officiant." Clara pulled her phone from her pocket, opened her Notes app, and began typing. "We could get married in the late morning and have a bridal lunch afterward. We can easily seat that small group on the porch or inside."

Kurt nodded, warming to the idea. "Let's have Johanson's Diner cater the food."

"That won't work."

"Why not?"

"Josef will insist on donating the food."

"You're right," he said, rubbing his chin. "I'll have to be firm and insist we pay him."

Clara grinned. "Good luck with that. I'll buy an arrangement for the table, and my bouquet and your boutonniere from the florist around the corner from Sweets & Treats. And I'll bake my own wedding cake."

"Are you sure?"

"Absolutely. I've always wanted to," Clara said. "And since it's a cake for only a handful of people, it'll be easy."

Kurt pulled his phone from his pocket and opened his calendar. "Let's pick the date."

They leaned over the screen, their heads touching.

"My trial ends three weeks from Wednesday," he said. "The Saturday after that is four weeks from today."

"Then that's our date," Clara said. "The last Saturday in October." She turned to him, beaming. "I love the sound of that."

"Me too." He pulled her into a long, leisurely kiss. The throw slipped from her shoulders, and he drew it back around her. "Look at us—we started out saying we didn't have time to plan a wedding, and, in fifteen minutes, we've done it. What have we overlooked?"

"We'll need an officiant."

"I know a judge who used to be a pastor," Kurt said. "I'll ask him."

"And wedding clothes," Clara added. "You have a closet full of beautiful suits. I'll have to buy a dress."

"Your wedding dress!" Kurt smacked his forehead with his palm. "How could I forget that? That's a big deal. Do you have enough time?"

"I'll find something," Clara said. "I love old-fashioned wedding dresses, and there's that new vintage store on the street behind the patisserie. They're open tomorrow —I'll stop in after church."

"What if they don't have anything? I don't want you to be stressed, hunting for a dress at the last minute."

"There's always online," Clara said with a shrug. "I've got plenty of time. For some reason, I feel confident my dress is out there. I'm not worried about settling for something second-best."

"I think we're set, then," Kurt said, wrapping his arms around her.

Noelle stirred, stood, and jumped to the ground. She gave herself a fierce shake, looked from Kurt to Clara, then trotted up the steps to the guesthouse Clara rented from Tabitha Trent.

"I think she's trying to tell us it's time to go in," Kurt said with a chuckle.

"It's like she waited for us to finish our wedding plans," Clara said. "I swear that dog understands English at a third-grade level."

Kurt rose and pulled Clara to her feet. "Knowing what I know about Noelle," he said, grinning, "I have to agree."

CHAPTER 3

Clara cupped her hands around her face and peered into the window of The Keepsake Closet while she waited for the shop to open. Circular racks filled with skirts, blouses, pants, jackets, and knee-length dresses occupied the center of the store. Along the right wall, tall racks stretched the length of the store —with winter coats toward the front, then long dresses in every color of the rainbow, and still more garments disappearing out of sight toward the rear.

On the left side, shelves of purses were arranged by color, neat as a pin. The front window display featured cozy fall sweaters—some cable-knit, others soft cashmere. A banner overhead proclaimed: Find Your One-of-a-Kind Treasure.

Clara knew she was there to find her wedding dress, but she made a mental note to try on the camel-colored cashmere turtleneck and the sapphire-blue cable-knit in the window. She bit her lip, and hoped there was a bridal section out of sight.

The heavy tumblers of the front door lock clicked, followed by the deep thunk of the deadbolt sliding free. A tall woman with blonde hair pulled into a high pony-tail opened the door, propped it with a stopper, and placed a doormat that read The Keepsake Closet in pink letters on a black background at the entrance to the shop.

Clara stepped away from the window and walked to the open door.

The woman looked up and smiled. "Good afternoon! Were you waiting for me?"

"I was," Clara said, extending her hand. "Clara Conway. I own Sweets & Treats on the next street."

"I'm Amy," the woman replied, shaking her hand. She looked to be in her thirties, like Clara. "Welcome to The Keepsake Closet. I love your bakery! Your pastries are delicious, of course, but your window displays are awe-inspiring. You've created such a welcoming shop. I hope I can emulate your example."

The two women crossed the threshold as strangers, and, within moments, felt like friends.

"That's kind of you to say," Clara said. "I'm afraid I left nose prints on your front window because I spent so much time gawking at the beautiful things in your shop.

You've merchandized this beautifully," she said, gesturing to the racks around her.

Amy's face lit up. "That means so much coming from you! What brings you in today? Are you looking for anything special?"

"As a matter of fact, I am." Clara moved toward the window display, Amy trailing beside her. "Do you mind if I take these two sweaters to try on?"

"Of course not!" Amy said. "So, you're shopping for fall and winter clothes?"

"Not exactly," Clara replied, smiling. "Those just caught my eye. I'm actually here to find …" She hesitated, still scarcely believing what she was about to say. "My wedding dress."

Amy clasped her hands over her heart. "Oh, my goodness! I love that. First—congratulations! That's wonderful. Second—when's the wedding?"

"Thank you," Clara said. "The last Saturday in October."

Amy's eyebrows shot up. "Oh! That's soon. What kind of dress are you looking for? I'm sorry to say we don't have any traditional bridal gowns at the moment. I hope to expand into bridal wear someday."

"I'm not looking for a traditional gown," Clara said. "This is a second marriage for both of us, and we only picked the date last night. It'll be a very small wedding. My fiancé owns property outside of town, and we're getting married at the newly restored farmhouse. I'd like something vintage—cream-colored—possibly lace. Long or midi length."

Amy furrowed her brow, thinking. "I have an off-white lace dress that might work. It's a size ten—probably big on you—but it could be taken in easily. I also have a satin sheath from the 1980s with rhinestones on the bodice."

"The rhinestone one doesn't sound like me," Clara said with a small laugh.

Amy scrutinized her up and down. "I agree—it doesn't seem like your style. But you never know until you try it on. I'll pull both for you. Oh—and there's an ivory satin pantsuit on one of the center racks that would look fabulous on you."

"Add that one, too," Clara said. "Do you mind if I browse a bit to see if anything else catches my eye?"

"I was going to suggest it," Amy said. "Take your time and let me know when you're ready."

Clara poked through the racks for the next twenty minutes, selecting a green velvet midi dress with an empire waist and a full skirt that shimmered from lime to emerald in the light, and a pair of red-and-black plaid wool trousers. She found Amy straightening handbags near the counter.

"You've got a good eye," Amy said approvingly. "That green dress will be stunning with your hair and skin tone." She led Clara to a curtained dressing room. "There's a three-way mirror right around the corner," she added, pointing. "Let me know if you need anything."

Clara kicked off her sneakers and set her jeans and T-shirt on the chair in the corner. The lace dress was exactly what she'd hoped to find. She unzipped it and slipped it over her head. Amy had been right—it was at least one size too large.

She smoothed it over her hips, zipped it, and looked at herself in the mirror. The woman staring back didn't smile. The square neckline wasn't flattering, and the lace scratched her skin even through the lining. Clara couldn't imagine spending an entire day in that dress.

The rhinestone-studded sheath fit better but made her look like she was headed to a Halloween party as Stephanie Mangano from *Saturday Night Fever*. "No way," she muttered, rehanging it carefully.

The pantsuit was too businesslike. She tried on both sweaters and the wool trousers next. They fit perfectly, and the prices were fair, so she folded them neatly and set them aside.

Her eyes fell on the velvet dress again. The label was designer—and the price tag made her hesitate. She didn't need a fancy dress. She wasn't going to get married in green velvet. But still … trying it on would be fun.

Clara pulled the sumptuous fabric over her head. It slipped into place as if it had been made for her. The rich velvet caressed her shoulders, draping perfectly over her frame. She turned to the mirror and inhaled sharply. Her auburn hair gleamed against the deep green fabric, and her eyes sparkled the same shade. She swept open the curtain and stepped toward the three-way mirror.

A woman browsing nearby looked up and gasped. "That dress looks absolutely stunning on you!"

Clara smiled. "It is pretty. I'm just not sure where I'd wear it."

"Honey," the woman said, "that's the perfect holiday dress. Are you married?"

"About to be," Clara replied.

"Then get that husband of yours to take you somewhere fancy. Better yet—on New Year's Eve! You'll be the most beautiful woman in the room."

Clara chuckled.

"I'm serious. Have you ever talked yourself out of buying a dress you loved because you didn't know where you'd wear it—and then later the occasion arose, and the dress was gone? You'd kick yourself for not buying it."

Clara nodded. "We've all done that."

"Exactly," the woman said. "That green number is one of those dresses."

Clara turned this way and that before the mirror. *She's right,* she thought. *I may not have found my wedding dress today, but I was meant to go home with this one.*

Back in the dressing room, she changed into her jeans and T-shirt, folded the velvet dress carefully, and carried her purchases to the register.

"Oh, good—you're getting the green one!" Amy said. "I almost brought it in to you earlier. I caught a glimpse of you in it—it's absolute perfection."

"Thank you," Clara said. "I love it. I hope I find a wedding dress I like as much."

"I'll keep an eye out for you," Amy said. "If you leave your number, I'll call if anything that fits your vision comes in."

"That would be so helpful," Clara said, pulling a Sweets & Treats business card from her purse. She flipped it over and wrote her cell number on the back.

Amy wrapped each item in tissue and placed them in a carrier bag. "Anytime you're looking for something in particular, let me know. I'll be happy to help."

"Thank you," Clara said. "I think you're going to be very successful here."

"That's the plan," Amy said with a smile.

"Are you a member of the Downtown Merchants Association?" Clara asked.

Amy shook her head.

"I'm on the board," Clara said. "You'll fit right in—the

merchants here support each other. I'll drop off an information packet for you. And please stop by the patisserie. I'd love to treat you to coffee and a pastry."

"That's kind of you," Amy said. "I'll take you up on that." Tilting her head, she added, "I'm sorry you didn't find your wedding dress here, but I have a strong feeling you'll find it soon—maybe even later today."

CHAPTER 4

Clara set the bakery boxes containing apple pies on her kitchen counter and carried her new clothes to the bedroom. The sunny afternoon had given way to thick gray clouds, the first sign of a rainy week ahead. By the time she'd arrived home, the temperature had dropped ten degrees.

She sorted through the shopping bag from The Keepsake Closet and pulled out the sapphire-blue cable-knit sweater, trading it for the T-shirt she'd been wearing. She and Kurt were having dinner that evening at Maisie and Josef's, and the cozy sweater would be perfect for the occasion.

On her way home, she had stopped at Sweets & Treats to retrieve the apple pie she was bringing for dessert, and brought home an extra one. Now, with both pies safely boxed on the counter, she reached for her coat.

Noelle, her faithful terrier mix who followed her like a heat-seeking missile, planted herself between Clara and the door.

"You want to go for a walk, don't you, girl?" Clara rubbed the dog's silky ears. "I'm sorry, but I don't think we'll have time today. We need to head over to see Laura, Ian, and Tabitha."

Noelle sat down and fixed Clara with an expectant gaze.

"Remember how Kurt and I decided we're getting married soon?" Clara asked.

Noelle's tail swept the floor in a slow wag.

"I'd like to stop by their house to tell them the news —and invite them to the wedding. I thought I'd bring them an apple pie, too."

Noelle gave a short woof of agreement.

"Kurt's picking me up for dinner at Maisie and Josef's in about an hour," Clara continued. "If I don't take you for a walk today, I promise we'll go for an extra-long one tomorrow. The patisserie's closed on Mondays, so I'll have plenty of time."

At that, Noelle leapt to her feet and spun in a happy circle.

Clara picked up the pie, and she and Noelle trotted up the sloping back lawn toward the three-story Victorian mansion occupied by Tabitha Trent, her grand-daughter Laura Ramsey, and Laura's teenage son, Ian. Clara climbed the steps and knocked before pushing the door open. It still amazed her that the people of Pinewood never locked their doors during the day.

"Laura?" Clara called as Noelle darted inside ahead of her.

"Noelle!" Ian's excited greeting echoed from the dining room.

Clara carried the pie through the kitchen and set it on the counter before stepping into the front parlor. High ceilings, elaborate carved moldings, and a marble fireplace spoke of the home's grand past. Even on a cloudy afternoon, the large bay window flooded the room with light.

Tabitha Trent sat in her chair by the window, pencil poised over the Sunday crossword. Laura lounged on the sofa, legs tucked beneath her, grading papers from her high-school chemistry class. Ian rolled on the floor with Noelle, ignoring his open textbooks on the dining room table.

"Clara, dear!" Tabitha folded her newspaper and reached for her cane.

"Don't get up," Clara said quickly, rushing to her side to kiss her cheek. "I should've called. I hope I'm not intruding."

"Not at all," Laura called out from the sofa, setting

aside her papers and swinging her legs to the floor. "I've been grading tests since lunch—I need a break. I'm happy to see you." She patted the sofa cushion beside her. "Come sit. Can I get you something to drink?"

"Thank you, but no. I can't stay long. Kurt and I are heading to Maisie and Josef's for an early dinner, but I wanted to share some news first."

Tabitha and Laura exchanged expectant glances while Ian and Noelle continued to play.

Clara began, "As you know, Kurt and I have been planning our wedding."

Laura nodded. "It sounds like it's going to be the biggest affair Pinewood has seen in years. Running your patisserie and organizing a big wedding—I don't know how you do it all!"

"That's just it," Clara said with a laugh. "We realized last night that we can't. We've decided not to have a big blowout wedding."

Tabitha leaned forward. "You're still getting married, though?"

"Absolutely," Clara said, smiling. "That's why I'm here. We're getting married on the last Saturday in October—at Bloom Cottage. Our ceremony will be at eleven, followed by lunch. We're only inviting ten people, and we'd love for the three of you to come."

"Oh, Clara!" Laura exclaimed, pulling her into a hug. "Of course we'll be there—won't we, Gran?"

"I'd love to come," Tabitha said. "But I'm not as spry as I used to be. I remember that property from decades ago, when my husband and I were friends with Kurt's grandparents. There wasn't even a driveway back then —I'm not sure I could manage the walk."

"You won't have to," Clara said quickly. "A driveway exists now, and Kurt is setting up a ramp for easy access to the farmhouse. We remodeled it—there's even a first-floor bathroom now."

"Then wild horses couldn't keep me away," Tabitha said, smiling.

"You only decided this last night?" Laura asked. "Have you got everything you need?"

"Almost," Clara said. "I'm looking for a dress. I went to The Keepsake Closet today."

"The new vintage clothing store downtown?" Laura asked. "It looks adorable when you drive by. I can't wait to go in."

"It's lovely," Clara said. "I got this sweater there this afternoon." She smoothed the sleeve. "I didn't find a wedding dress, but I picked up another sweater, a pair of slacks, and a gorgeous holiday dress."

"My wedding gown is still my favorite garment," Tabitha said. "You can see it in that photo on the mantel." She pointed. "The one on the left is my wedding portrait; the photo on the right is my sister and her husband."

Clara crossed to the mantel. "I've admired these before," she said, picking up the picture of Tabitha and her husband. "You both look stunning. I love the simplicity of your satin gown—the fitted bodice flowing into that cascading skirt. Very chic! It has long sleeves—was it cold when you got married?"

"December fifteenth," Tabitha replied. "We said our vows at five-thirty and held the reception at a hotel nearby. A blizzard hit, and everyone got snowed in. The party lasted all night. My father said as long as the champagne flowed, no one would mind—and he was right."

"Sounds like quite an adventure," Clara said, setting the photo back and picking up the other one. "Your sister's dress looks different—almost like something from the 1920s. Did she wear a vintage gown?"

Tabitha shook her head. "She was my half-sister, and twenty-five years older. That photo was taken in 1928."

Clara studied it closely. "Her dress looks straight out of *The Great Gatsby*. It's gorgeous."

"I wasn't even born when she married," Tabitha said softly. "I idolized her. She was glamorous, kind, and … died of cancer when I was ten. It broke everyone's heart."

Clara returned the photo to the mantel with care. "It's a beautiful picture."

"Do you like her dress?" Tabitha asked.

"Oh my gosh, yes," Clara said. "It's absolutely breath-taking. I love the symmetry of the Art Déco lace overlay on the bodice and the way the beaded fringe forms little cap sleeves and falls from the dropped waist. It looks like it would be so much fun to wear."

"You can't tell from the photo," Tabitha said, "but that fringe was made from rows of tiny glass beads."

"No kidding?" Clara returned to study it.

"That thing weighed a ton," Tabitha said with a laugh.

"What sort of dress are you hoping to find?" Laura asked.

"I'd love a form-fitting sheath like your sister's," Clara said. "Nothing ball-gown or mermaid style. The geometric Art Déco lace in her dress really appeals to me—something understated but elegant. More elevated than an ivory cocktail dress."

Tabitha exchanged a glance with Laura, who nodded, then cleared her throat. "So … would you like a dress like my sister's—if you could find one?"

"Definitely!" Clara said. "It's exactly what I hoped to find at The Keepsake Closet. I doubt I'll come across something like it before my wedding, but even a dress with that cut—or beaded fringe—would be a dream come true."

Tabitha's grin softened her wrinkles. "We might just be able to help with that. There's a trunk of my sister's old clothes in the attic." She glanced upward. "I'm sure her wedding dress is there, along with some other beautiful pieces. If her gown doesn't fit or suit you, one of the others might."

Clara stared at her. "You mean …?"

"It would give me great joy to see you married in my sister's wedding dress," Tabitha said gently. "But only if you truly love it. Admiring a dress in a photo is one thing—seeing it on your own body is another."

Clara blinked rapidly, fighting sudden tears.

"We'll take that as a yes," Laura said, rising. "Ian and I will go up to the attic and bring the trunk down."

Clara's smartwatch vibrated with a text from Kurt: *Be there soon.*

"This is so incredibly kind of you," she said. "Would you mind if I came back tomorrow to look through the trunk? Kurt's on his way to pick me up."

"Even better," Tabitha said. "I'll be around all day, and we can take our time."

"I can hardly wait," Clara said, wiping at her eyes. "This is so exciting."

"I'm tempted to call in sick so I can be here, too," Laura said with a laugh.

"You never take time off work," Tabitha teased. "Why don't you? And Clara—invite Maisie to come. I know she'd love to be part of it."

"I will," Clara said, smiling. "I hope you can be there, Laura. You're like family to me."

Kurt's SUV turned into the driveway. "Noelle and I had better go." She turned toward the kitchen. "I left an apple pie on the counter for you."

"Can she spend the afternoon with me?" Ian asked. "I'll take her for a walk and bring her to the guest house after dinner."

"She'd love that," Clara said. "Thank you—*all* of you—for everything."

"Ten o'clock tomorrow?" Tabitha asked.

"Perfect," Clara said, nodding as she headed for the door.

CHAPTER 5

Josef Johanson reached for his wife's empty plate and stacked it on top of his own. "You know the rule," he said, pushing back his chair and rising from the table. "If you cook, you don't clean up."

"I won't argue with that," Maisie replied with a grin.

Kurt stood and reached for Clara's plate. "You made the apple pie," he said, smiling at her. "So that applies to you, too."

"At least let me help clear the table," Clara protested.

"Not on your life," Josef said firmly. "You two just got started talking about this wedding. Go into the living room—we'll join you when we're done."

Clara and Maisie exchanged amused glances, then rose and left the dining room without further argument.

"I'll load the dishwasher and wash," Kurt offered. "You dry."

"Sounds like a plan," Josef said. The two men slipped into their familiar rhythm, working in comfortable silence as the sound of clinking dishes and running water filled the kitchen.

When Kurt rinsed the last pot and handed it to Josef, the older man paused before speaking. "Maisie and I couldn't be happier that you're marrying Clara," he said quietly. "I knew there was something special about her the moment she walked into Johanson's Diner. The way she jumped in to help us during the holiday rush told me everything I needed to know about her character. And that she accepted that cooking job—considering her skills and experience—was impressive."

Kurt smiled. "That's what I thought, too. She was stranded in Pinewood, waiting for parts to fix her fancy foreign SUV. She wasn't in any kind of financial trouble—she didn't have to work."

Josef nodded. "She did it because she loves to cook. And she recognized that Maisie and I needed help."

Kurt turned and leaned against the sink, drying his hands on a towel. "I wasn't looking to fall in love when I met Clara," he said. "I never thought I'd find someone to share my life with after Rachel died."

Josef placed the pot in a cabinet and looked at him. "You made our daughter very happy, Kurt. You were like a son to us then, and you've continued to be one ever since."

Kurt hesitated. "Do you or Maisie ever have second thoughts about my marriage to Clara? Do you feel like I'm forgetting Rachel?"

Josef shook his head.

"I'll always love her," Kurt continued. "Not a day goes by that I don't think about her."

"The same is true for both of us, son," Josef said gently. "But that doesn't mean we can't love Clara, too. Love isn't finite—it's endless. The more you give, the more you have to give."

Kurt pressed his lips into a thin line and swallowed hard.

Josef drew a deep breath and squared his shoulders. "I never told you about the conversation Rachel had with Maisie and me the week before she passed," he said.

"When she was in hospice?" Kurt asked.

Josef nodded. "She knew her time was short. She told me you were the love of her life—and that your marriage was everything she'd hoped for. She said you were a perfect husband." His voice broke slightly; then he gave a small laugh. "She called you a 'we' person—someone who is happiest as part of a couple."

Kurt turned his face aside, blinking back emotion.

"She made us promise something," Josef continued. "She wanted you to remarry someday. Rachel didn't want you to spend years grieving her. She told us the best way to honor her memory was to keep living fully. She even said she'd prayed for God to send you a new soulmate—someone we'd love like a daughter, and who would take care of us in our old age." Josef inhaled deeply. "She made us promise we'd encourage you when you found her."

Kurt stepped forward and pulled the older man into a tight embrace. "You've kept your promise," he whispered.

Josef patted him on the back, then pulled away, his eyes glistening.

"Thank you for telling me this," Kurt said, his voice rough. "It means more than you know."

"Rachel would've loved Clara," Josef said simply. "We all do."

CHAPTER 6

Clara opened her eyes the next morning, caught between sleepiness and excitement. She glanced at her bedside clock. Four forty-five a.m. counted as sleeping in on a weekday.

She and Kurt had talked until after eleven the night before—about their wedding plans, their evening with Maisie and Josef, even where they would live after they were married. But when the hour grew late, they decided that topic could wait. Kurt had to be in court at 8:30.

She'd assumed she'd sleep in. Instead, Clara rolled onto her side and buried her face in the pillow. The image of the dress in the photo refused to fade. Finally, she threw back the covers and got up. She had five hours before meeting Maisie and Tabitha, and her mind was buzzing. She needed to do something—anything—to keep herself busy.

After letting Noelle out for a quick comfort break, she fed her dog and launched into a full deep-clean of the guest house. She'd finished by 7:30—floors vacuumed, counters wiped, laundry folded. She showered, applied her makeup, and styled her hair. She wanted to look her best when she tried on the dress.

It was still only 8:45. She clipped Noelle's leash to her collar, grabbed her jacket, and the two of them headed out into the gray morning. The air smelled faintly of rain, and low clouds pressed down on the rooftops. Although the skies threatened, Clara and Noelle walked briskly for nearly an hour. They were only two houses away from home when the drizzle began. She quickened her pace, returned Noelle to the cottage, and was crossing the back lawn toward the big house when Maisie's car pulled into Tabitha's driveway.

The two women climbed the porch steps together, the aroma of coffee and cinnamon growing stronger with each step. They let themselves in.

Laura was in the kitchen, pulling trays of golden-brown cinnamon and currant scones from the oven.

"Those smell fabulous," Clara said.

Laura set the trays on the counter, then turned to hug her. "I'm so glad you're here," she said, embracing first Clara, then Maisie.

"I thought you were kidding about calling in sick," Clara said.

"I have lots of unused PTO," Laura replied, laughing. "I called my favorite substitute teacher last night. She was thrilled to teach my class. Her husband's been out of work, so she was grateful for the hours. Win-win."

"That's terrific," Clara said.

"Grandma's in the parlor," Laura added. "Neither of us slept well last night, so we've been up since the crack of dawn."

Clara chuckled. "Same here."

"That makes four of us," Maisie said.

"Let's wait on coffee and scones until after you see the dress," Laura said. "Ian and I brought the trunk into the parlor last night, and I found the gown this morning. I put it on top. You'll want to see the other garments in there, too—they're beautiful."

Maisie clasped her hands together. "I'd love that!"

Laura led them into the parlor. A large trunk sat in the center of the room, its leather corners scuffed, and its brass hinges dulled with age. A faint hint of cedar hung in the air. The lid stood open, revealing layers of yellowed tissue paper.

"Good morning, Tabitha," Clara said, heading toward the older woman, who sat ensconced in her favorite chair.

"Say hello to me later," Tabitha said, eyes sparkling. "I can't wait a moment longer for you to see that dress."

Clara walked to the trunk, Laura and Maisie hovering close behind. She lifted the wrapped garment from the top and carried it to the sofa. Carefully peeling back the tissue layers, she inhaled sharply.

The dress was breathtaking—long layers of beaded trim falling from a dropped waist, geometric embroidery stretching from shoulder to hip, and tiny cap sleeves fashioned from rows of glass-bead fringe. The ivory silk gleamed faintly, even in the soft morning light.

As Clara eyed the dress in wonder, each of the other three women gasped.

Tabitha called from her chair, "It's even lovelier than I remembered."

"The embroidery is exquisite," Clara murmured. She peered inside the gown. "The silk lining is in perfect shape. And not a blemish or stain anywhere." She held it at arm's length, admiring both sides. "It's incredible."

"Would you like to try it on?" Tabitha asked.

"Absolutely."

"You can use the dining room," Tabitha said, smiling.

Clara carried the gown reverently into the dining room and laid it across the table. She slipped out of her tennis shoes, joggers, and sweatshirt, then lifted the dress over her head. The fabric whispered against her skin as it settled perfectly into place—light, fluid, and surprisingly comfortable. It felt like it had been waiting for her.

The bodice hugged her curves without constriction. The fringe swayed gently as she moved, the weight of the beading giving the gown just enough heft to drape beautifully. She straightened her shoulders, drew a steady breath, and walked to the parlor with the cadence of a bride walking down the aisle.

Maisie and Laura turned mid-conversation. Both froze, their mouths falling open.

Tabitha's hand flew to her heart. For a moment, no one spoke.

Clara stood in the doorway, uncertain, looking from one face to another.

Maisie finally reached for a tissue and dabbed her eyes. "You are an absolute vision," she whispered.

"You wouldn't find a more beautiful dress, even if you tried on every one within a thousand miles," Laura said.

"It's perfect," Tabitha agreed. "My sister was married on a chilly day in March. My mother always said the fringe on her dress shimmered like frost on the grass when she walked down the aisle."

"The mirror in the foyer will give you a full-length view," Laura said.

Clara crossed the room, the fringe swinging gracefully around her hips. When she reached the mirror, her breath caught.

The scooped neckline framed her slender neck, and the loose curls of her auburn hair brushed her shoulders at just the right spot. The ivory silk glowed against her skin, and the geometric lace seemed made for her. She'd never applied the word exquisite to herself before—but now, it fit.

She tore her gaze away from the mirror and returned to the others, her heart racing.

"So," Maisie asked softly, "are you saying yes to the dress?"

Clara smiled through sudden tears. "Yes," she said, her voice trembling. "A million times *YES*."

LATER THAT AFTERNOON, after the four friends had enjoyed their scones and coffee—and had oohed and aahed over the treasures in the trunk—Tabitha had retreated to her room for a nap, and Maisie had gone home, saying Tabitha had the right idea.

"These garments are priceless," Clara said, looking around the parlor. "I'll help you pack them away."

"You don't have to do that," Laura replied. "I'll finish up."

"I'd love to handle them again," Clara said with a smile. "Besides, there's something I'd like to ask you."

She crossed to the sofa, where dresses, skirts, coats, and trousers lay draped across the cushions. Turning to Laura, she hesitated for just a moment before speaking. "I know it's a small wedding, but I'd still like to have a friend stand up with me. Would you be my matron of honor?"

Laura took a step forward and threw her arms around Clara. "I was hoping you'd ask me! You're like the sister I never had—but always wanted. I'd be honored."

Clara hugged her tightly in return. "Thank you. You can wear whatever you'd like, but ..." She leaned over the sofa, shifting garments until she pulled out a deep purple satin A-line dress. "I saw you linger over this one earlier. Would you like to wear it at my wedding? It looks like it'll be your size."

Laura's jeans and T-shirt were on the floor in record time.

"Here," Clara laughed, holding the dress open and slipping it over Laura's head.

Just as the wedding gown had seemed made for Clara, this one fit Laura perfectly.

Clara gasped. "Whether you wear it to my wedding or not, you need to keep this dress. It's stunning—it deserves to be worn, not packed away in tissue."

Laura went to the mirror in the foyer, and Clara followed her. Their eyes met in their reflection.

"I can't wait until Gran wakes up and I show her this," Laura said, smiling. "She's going to be thrilled."

Clara grinned. "I'm convinced this was all meant to be."

They returned to the parlor, and Clara helped Laura out of the dress. Together, they began folding the garments spread across the sofa, carefully tucking each one back into its protective tissue paper.

"Can I ask you something?" Laura said as they worked.

"Of course," Clara replied.

"Have you decided where you're going to live once you're married?"

Clara sighed. "We talked about it a little last night. Bloom Cottage is too far out of town for me to commute to the patisserie in the early morning, and the guest house is too small—especially once we start a family."

"So, you'll be living at Kurt's?"

Clara pressed her lips into a thin line. "That's the question. His house is on the other side of town—too far for me to get to work easily. And ..." She lifted her eyes to Laura's. "He and Rachel built it together. It's a beautiful home, don't get me wrong, but it doesn't feel like me."

"Have you told him that?"

Clara nodded slowly. "I think he loves that house. It's perfect for him. He's a little disappointed, but we agreed to look for something in this area."

"That may take a while," Laura said. "Houses don't often change hands here."

"Would you mind if we continued renting the guest house until we find one?" Clara asked.

"Of course not," Laura said warmly. "You're our favorite tenant of all time. Stay as long as you'd like." She hesitated, then smiled. "Actually, I have a favor to ask, too."

Clara raised an eyebrow. "Shoot."

"I'm attending a chemistry teachers' workshop in the first week of November," Laura said. "I've been invited to be on a panel."

"That's wonderful!" Clara said. "Congratulations."

"It's in Chicago, and I'll be gone for four nights. Gran and Ian will stay home. I'm sure they'll be fine, but …"

"You'd feel better knowing I was close by," Clara finished for her. "That way I can check on them."

Laura nodded. "Exactly. I just assumed you'd still be in the guest house when I agreed to participate."

"Kurt and I will stay there while you're gone," Clara said. "Even if you hadn't mentioned it, I would've offered. I'll feel better about it, too."

"Do you think Kurt will mind?" Laura asked.

"Absolutely not," Clara said with a laugh. "For all I know, he'll be out of town on business that week. And honestly, I'm more comfortable there, anyway."

Laura let out a sigh of relief and folded the last dress. "Thank you. That gives me such peace of mind."

"My pleasure," Clara smiled warmly. "That's what sisters of the heart are for."

CHAPTER 7

*L*aura left her car idling by the front door. She hurried up the front steps and found Tabitha sitting in her chair by the window. Her grandmother, wearing her wool coat, Sunday hat, and white cotton gloves, clutched her pocketbook in her lap.

"I'm sorry I'm late, Gran," Laura said. "A parent meeting ran long. I see you're ready to go. We'll still make it to the bank before it closes."

"Would you mind bringing that package on the end table?" Tabitha asked, glancing at the small parcel wrapped in gold paper and tied with a burgundy ribbon. "Robert has managed my accounts for decades, and he's done a wonderful job. It's been a blessing to work with someone I have complete confidence in. I want to thank him personally and acknowledge his retirement with a small gift."

"That's so thoughtful, Gran," Laura said, picking up the package. She followed behind as Tabitha grasped her cane and made her way out the front door, hesitating at the top step.

Laura caught up and offered her arm. Together, they made their way—step by careful step—down to the car.

They arrived at the downtown branch of Pinewood Bank ten minutes before closing time. Everyone there knew Tabitha. She conducted all of her banking in person and treated each visit as an important occasion. To say she was a legend at the bank was an understatement.

Heads turned as Tabitha marched through the double doors, posture erect, head held high, employing her cane in regal fashion. She greeted each employee by name as she crossed the lobby toward Robert's glasswalled office at the rear of the bank.

Robert hurried out to meet her. "Hello, Mrs. Trent," he said.

She paused, transferred her cane to her left hand, and extended her right.

"I'm surprised to see you," he continued. "We reviewed your portfolio with my replacement last week. I hope nothing's wrong."

"Not in the least," Tabitha said. "I have great confidence that Patricia will take excellent care of me, just as you have all these years."

"I'm glad to hear it," Robert said. "And Catherine will remain with the bank as Patricia's assistant. She's as familiar with your portfolio as I am."

"Good to know," Tabitha replied. "You remember my granddaughter, Laura Ramsey?"

"Of course," Robert said, shaking Laura's hand. "Nice to see you."

"She does that newfangled online banking," Tabitha said with a hint of mischief, "so she never has the pleasure of coming into the bank and seeing you people. I didn't know if you'd remember each other."

"For heaven's sake, Gran," Laura said, rolling her eyes. "I've been banking here for decades, too. Of course, Robert and I—and the rest of the staff—know each other."

"I've noticed online transactions from your accounts," Robert said.

"Laura's done those for me," Tabitha said. "I know where to find the …," she turned to Laura. "What do you call it, again?"

"User name and password," Laura supplied.

"Yes." Tabitha snapped her fingers. "I've got them written down on a paper at the bottom of the drawer in the end table by my chair. Laura insists I might need them someday, but I never intend to." Tabitha returned her cane to her right hand and continued into Robert's office. His desktop was bare except for a telephone. He had cleared away the photos, trophies, and plaques from his long career. In their place stood a bouquet of flowers and a rainbow-striped Mylar balloon bearing the words Congratulations on Your Retirement! An oversized yellow smiley-face balloon bobbed beside it. On his credenza sat the remnants of a half-eaten sheet cake in a bakery box.

Robert pulled out a chair for Tabitha and she lowered herself into it. Laura took the seat beside her grandmother, and Robert sat behind his desk across from them.

"Would either of you like a piece of cake?" he asked, gesturing toward the box behind him.

Both women declined.

"How can we help you?" Robert asked, waving in Patricia and Catherine, who had gathered outside his office door.

Tabitha greeted them warmly. "Good heavens, I didn't mean to disrupt everyone. I know this is your last day, Robert, and I wanted to mark the occasion and thank you for your decades of guidance and friendship. I know you're leaving me in good hands." She smiled at Patricia and then at Catherine. Reaching toward Laura, she took the wrapped package.

"I've enjoyed talking with you about your rare book collection over the years," Tabitha said. "As you know, my late husband shared your interest and had quite a collection himself." She handed the package to Robert. "I thought this volume would find a good home with you."

Robert leaned back in his chair, visibly taken aback. "This is very kind of you—and unexpected," he said. "Working with you has been one of the highlights of my career." He looked at the beautiful package in his hands. "It feels like a book. May I open it?"

A smile played on Tabitha's lips. "Certainly."

Robert untied the ribbon and loosened the tape.

Tabitha sat a little straighter and leaned forward while Patricia and Catherine took a step closer to watch.

The wrapping paper slipped to the desk, revealing a small, compact volume. The binding was cinnamon-colored ribbed cloth. A gilt wreath surrounded the title —also in gold, though faded with age.

Robert gasped when he read the words, staring wide-eyed at Tabitha.

Patricia and Catherine stepped even closer. Laura turned to her grandmother, her own breath catching.

"I feel like I should be wearing gloves to examine this," Robert said. He carefully opened to the two-color title page, then examined the hand-colored plate on the left.

"This is *Mr. Fezziwig's Ball,* by John Leech." His voice was full of reverence as he continued reading. "*A Christmas Carol. In Prose. A Ghost Story of Christmas.* By Charles Dickens."

He turned the volume toward them. "This illustration shows a young Scrooge celebrating with his coworkers," he said. He took a deep breath and looked at Tabitha. "This is an 1843 first edition, isn't it?"

She nodded. "I knew you'd recognize it instantly."

He brought a hand to his forehead. "This is an incredibly valuable volume."

"It's not in perfect shape, unfortunately," Tabitha said. "Someone tore out one of the illustrations, and there are stains on two pages."

"Even so," Robert said, "it's still far more than I can accept as a bank employee."

Tabitha smiled and tapped her watch. "Today was your last day, correct?"

"Yes."

"And the bank is closed for business? I believe someone locked the doors while we've been chatting."

"That's true," Catherine chimed in.

"Then you're no longer a bank employee," Tabitha said. "You're an old and dear friend."

He looked at her, speechless.

Tabitha grasped her cane and rose. "And now," she said, "Laura and I must be going. I'm sure your wife is waiting for you to come home to celebrate."

Robert stood as well. "I don't know what to say. Thank you so much, Mrs. Trent. I'll treasure this— always."

Tabitha patted his arm as she headed for the door. "May you have a long, healthy, and happy retirement." With that, she and Laura started toward the exit.

Catherine hurried after them. "I'll unlock the door for you," she said.

At the doorway, she turned back to Tabitha and Laura. "That was the nicest thing you could've done for him, Mrs. Trent. As he said, you'll be well taken care of by Patricia—and I'm always here to help you, too."

"Thank you, dear," Tabitha said. "I'll see you at my regular appointment next month."

CHAPTER 8

An intermittent breeze chased orange and gold leaves along the sidewalk in front of Sweets & Treats. Clara and Joan sat together at the small desk in the workroom, hunched over Clara's laptop.

"I think we've discussed every angle and possibility," Clara said. "It's time to place our supply order for the holiday season. Do you think we're being too optimistic?" She glanced over her shoulder toward the front of the shop. "We haven't had a customer since right after lunch."

"Honestly," Joan said, "I think we'll end up buying more of the basics at the last minute—and for higher prices. Once the weather turns cold, our sales will pick up. Nothing is as comforting as homemade bread, pastries, pies, and cakes when it's chilly outside."

Clara chuckled. "I guess I should be glad the weather turned this morning and that storm's rolling in."

"Exactly," Joan said. "Now, are you going to hit send on that order?"

Clara tapped her keyboard just as the bell over the front door jingled.

Joan laughed. "Didn't I tell you this weather would bring in business?"

Clara closed her laptop and rose to greet their customer. She stepped into the storefront and smiled as Kurt walked toward her.

"Hello, princess," he said, coming around the retail counter and pulling her in for a kiss.

"What are you doing here?" she asked. "I thought you were in trial the entire week."

"We settled," he said, grinning. "Right after the lunch break. Our witness this morning was devastating to their case."

"That's terrific," she said.

"It sure is. The other side's drafting the settlement agreement, and I suddenly have an afternoon free."

She leaned back in his arms and looked up at him. "What do you have in mind?"

"I've been thinking about Bloom Cottage," he said. "I know we talked about renting a table and chairs for our wedding lunch, but wouldn't it be nice to have some real furniture there, too?"

Clara stepped back and held up her hands. "I'm so sorry, Kurt. I wish that were possible, but we don't have time to furnish a house right now."

"I know," Kurt said, drawing her back to him. "I was thinking we could move some of the furniture from my house to the cottage. We've already decided we'll eventually sell my place, and we won't need all my furniture for staging. I stopped by to see if you think any of my stuff would work in the cottage. My schedule will inevitably fill up again, but for now I've suddenly got ten days free. I could move a few things out there—it'd make the cottage more comfortable for everyone at the wedding."

Clara tilted her head, considering. "You know what?" she said. "That's a great idea. We just finished placing our holiday supply order, so I can sneak out early."

"I was hoping you'd say that." Kurt smiled. "Want to come to my place and pick out what goes to the cottage?"

"Absolutely!"

KURT SET the lamp on the floor of the hallway beside the other two lined up near the door to his garage. "You made short work of that," he said with a grin.

"That's because most of your furniture is too big for

the small rooms at Bloom Cottage," Clara replied. "The leather sofa and chair from your home office, your guest bed, nightstand, and chest of drawers—plus these three lamps—are all the right scale and style. They'll suit the house perfectly."

"I'm glad you know this stuff," he said. "Is there anything else you'd really like to have out there?"

"I don't think so," she said. "I wish either your breakfast room or dining room table would fit."

"Me too," he said.

"They're both round, though, and that kitchen needs a rectangle. Plus, they're too modern. I'd like to find a simple farmhouse table." She wandered into the living room, taking one last look around. "We may want more of this later, but let's see how what we've picked out works and take it from there."

Kurt checked his watch. "One more idea. That big antiques mall by the highway is open until six. I'm not suggesting a marathon shopping spree, but we might get lucky and find that farmhouse table. If not, we'll rent a table as planned."

Clara smiled. "I've always wanted to stop in there. We have nothing else planned. Let's go."

Thirty minutes after the official closing time, they walked out of the antiques mall with a long, itemized receipt and a promise from the proprietor to call first thing in the morning about delivery.

Kurt took Clara's hand as they headed for his SUV. "I learned something very important this afternoon," he said solemnly.

Clara tipped her head, eyebrows arched. "Oh? What's that?"

"Never go into an antiques mall with you thinking it's going to be a quick—or cheap—trip."

Clara laughed. "We just got lucky! They had everything we wanted. I knew the minute we walked in and spotted the perfect farmhouse table that we were onto something."

He chuckled. "I'll give you that. It was a great find."

"I still had to walk through the rest of the store, though—to make sure."

"Of course," he said. "Due diligence."

"And then we came across that bedroom set we both loved—it'll be perfect for the cottage."

"True."

"Plus, there's no overhead lighting, so we needed lamps."

"A dozen lamps," he said dryly.

"Yep. A dozen."

"And rugs. Side tables. And an outdoor table and chairs."

"Sure," she said, grinning. "Plus, some art for the walls."

They reached his SUV, and he opened the door for her.

"You're not really upset, are you?" she asked, searching his face.

"Not at all," he said, eyes warm. "Just amazed at how quickly we managed to furnish an entire house."

"It's wonderful, isn't it? Once everything's delivered and in place, it'll look beautiful for the wedding."

He shut her door, crossed in front of the SUV, and slid behind the wheel.

As she buckled her seat belt, Clara touched his arm. "Oh! I bet the company delivering the antiques could pick up the furniture from your house. Then you won't have to rent a truck or haul it yourself."

"That's a brilliant idea," Kurt said. "It'll make things so much easier."

"There you go."

He laughed. "Makes it worth every penny we spent. Honestly, other than buying a new car, I don't think I've ever spent this much money in under three hours."

"I haven't either," Clara said with a teasing smile. "This isn't a regular occurrence for me."

He shot her a sideways glance. "You know what I think we should do now?"

"Head to my place so I can make grilled-cheese sandwiches for dinner—since we blew our wad on furniture?"

"Wrong," he said. "I'd like to take you to dinner to celebrate."

"I wasn't expecting that reaction."

"I'm amazed at how decisive you are—and at how much Clara Conway can get done when she puts her mind to it."

CHAPTER 9

"**A**re you sure you don't want any more of this?" Kurt gestured toward the three remaining slices of sausage and pepperoni pizza, their edges curling slightly in the cooling air.

Clara shook her head, smiling. "I'm so keyed up about our wedding tomorrow, I couldn't eat another bite."

"Are you sorry we didn't wait to have a big wedding like we'd originally planned?" he asked. "Our rehearsal dinner certainly wouldn't have been takeout pizza."

She reached for his hands, threading her fingers through his. "Not one bit," she said softly. "I couldn't be happier."

Kurt stood, still holding her hands, and pulled her to her feet. He wrapped his arms around her, drawing her close.

"And are you still happy with our decision?" she asked, her voice barely above a whisper.

"Completely," he said. "I'm off to Bloom Cottage, so you can get some sleep."

"I'm not sure how much sleep I'll get," she admitted with a laugh, "but I'll try. There are pastries from Sweets & Treats in the kitchen for your breakfast tomorrow—and ours on Sunday. I also stopped at the store for milk, eggs, butter, and coffee."

He grinned. "You plan to cook the day after our wedding? I thought we'd go into town for food."

"There's no way I'm leaving the cottage on Sunday," she said. "We'll have leftovers from the wedding lunch, too. If I have my way, we'll spend the whole day in bed."

Kurt chuckled. "I'm one hundred percent in favor of that." He followed her into the kitchen, watching her move easily through the space.

"Do you want to take this pizza with you in case you get hungry later?"

He shook his head. "I'm stuffed."

"Then let's drop it off for Ian on your way out," Clara said. "I'm sure he'd love it."

"Teenage boys are bottomless pits," Kurt said with a grin. "Isn't it a little late to disturb them?"

"I have a key," she replied. "We'll leave it in the fridge, and I'll text Ian that it's there."

They stepped closer, and, in the next moment, the

world around them seemed to fall away. Their kiss was slow and deep, full of promise and everything that waited for them tomorrow.

"It's a good thing we'll be married this time tomorrow," Kurt murmured, reluctantly breaking the kiss.

Clara nodded, breathless, her cheeks flushed. Noelle sat at their feet, tail thumping softly against the floor as if in approval.

Kurt gathered the groceries while Clara picked up the pizza box. Together, they stepped out into the cool evening and walked up the hill, their shadows long and intertwined, carrying their clandestine gift toward the large house.

CHAPTER 10

*L*aura and Ian tapped on Clara's door before seven the next morning.

Clara greeted them wearing sweatpants, a hoodie, and tennis shoes, Noelle's leash in one hand. The dog pranced at her feet.

"Good morning," Clara said. "Have I lost track of time?" She turned up the cuff of her hoodie to check her watch. "I thought we weren't headed to the salon for another half hour. I was going to take Noelle for a quick walk."

"My cousin called and asked if we could come in thirty minutes early for our hair and makeup," Laura said. "Didn't you get my text?"

"Oh gosh," Clara said. "I haven't even checked my phone. I'm so sorry—I'm all discombobulated." She looked down at her puppy, who gazed up with pleading eyes. "I'm sorry, sweet girl," she said. "Not today."

"That's okay," Ian interjected. "That's why I came with Mom. I'll take her for her morning walk and then bring her back to our house since she's spending the weekend with us."

"That's awfully nice of you," Clara said, handing him the leash.

"Thanks for leaving me that pizza last night," Ian said with a grin. "I was starving, and it was really good."

Clara sank to her knees and cupped Noelle's face in her hands. "I'm only going to be gone a couple of days," she murmured. "You'll be with Ian, and I know you won't even miss me—but I'll miss you a ton." She kissed the top of the dog's head. "I'm sorry you can't come to the wedding, but you'll be with us every other time we go to Bloom Cottage from now on."

Noelle swished her tail and pranced in place, eager to end the conversation and start her walk.

Clara rose, gave her beloved dog one last pat, and the four of them set out, Noelle leading the way.

LAURA HELD the vintage wedding gown open for Clara to step into. Together, they carefully pulled the dress up over Clara's hips to her shoulders.

"It's a good thing you're so slim," Laura said with a laugh, "or we'd have had to put this on over your head and risk messing up your hair."

Clara stepped in front of the full-length mirror in her bedroom as Laura fastened the tiny, silk-covered buttons up the back.

"My hair is perfect," Clara said, studying her reflection. "Your cousin did an amazing job. The style complements the dress, but it still looks modern and fresh." She caught Laura's eye in the mirror. "Thank you for bringing the photo of the dress with us this morning. Your cousin said it helped her decide on my hairstyle. I figured I'd wear my hair in loose curls around my shoulders."

"That would've been beautiful, too," Laura said.

"This half-up style is exactly what the dress needs," Clara replied. She rested one hand on the bed as she slipped on her shoes. "Would you mind taking a photo of me before we leave? We decided not to hire a photographer, since everyone has a cell phone with a decent camera. But now that we're here, on the day, I kind of wish we had."

Laura grabbed her phone and directed Clara into position before snapping a few photos. "I'd like to take a few more by the front door when we walk up to get Ian and Gran. It'll make a beautiful backdrop."

"Thank you," Clara said, reaching for Laura's phone. "Now I want to get one of you in your dress."

Laura smoothed the skirt of her simple satin gown. "It isn't elaborate," she said, "but it certainly is beautiful."

"That deep purple is your color," Clara said, gesturing for Laura to angle herself away from the camera and look toward the window. "That's perfect—hold it." She snapped several pictures.

Laura's phone vibrated in Clara's hand, and she passed it back.

"It's Ian," Laura said, glancing at the screen. "He says Gran's getting antsy. She doesn't want us to be late." Laura laughed. "It's not like they're going to start the wedding without the bride."

"No," Clara said, "but I agree with Tabitha—it's bad form to make people wait." She slipped out of her satin heels and into a pair of flats. "I'm not walking on the grass in my wedding shoes."

"Good thinking," Laura said, and the two of them set off.

Tabitha and Ian were waiting for them on the front porch.

"Ian's going to take photos of you by our front door," Tabitha said. "With his talent for framing, they'll be beautiful."

Laura and Clara exchanged smiles. "Great minds," Laura said.

Ian took a series of photos as the women stood together. The three of them leaned over his shoulder as he scrolled through the images.

"A professional couldn't have done any better," Clara said. "Thank you." She turned to Tabitha. "Doesn't Laura look spectacular in this purple number that belonged to your sister?"

Tabitha pulled a lace-edged hanky from her pocketbook and dabbed at her eyes. "She certainly does," she said. "You both take my breath away. I feel my sister's presence—and she's thrilled."

Laura sniffed, and Clara blinked rapidly, trying not to cry.

Ian looked at the three of them. "We'd better get out of here before you're all bawling," he said.

Tabitha laughed. "I think you're right. I only wish there was going to be a single gentleman at the wedding to see Laura in that dress." She smiled at her granddaughter. "You know what they say—people often meet their future spouse at a wedding."

"Oh, Gran," Laura groaned, rolling her eyes as she and Ian helped her down the steps to the waiting car. "It's a very small wedding. I think you'd better get that idea out of your head."

Clara followed in their wake, smiling to herself. There *was* going to be a single gentleman at the wedding

—Kurt's best man, Brad—and he was the right age. She kept that information to herself but sent up a silent prayer.

65

CHAPTER 11

Laura drove slowly up the driveway to Bloom Cottage.

"Duck!" Tabitha called to Clara, who sat in the front seat beside Laura. "Kurt and everyone else are on the front porch. We don't want them to see you!"

"Oh, Gran," Laura started to protest.

"It's bad luck!" Tabitha said firmly.

"That's an old wives' tale," Laura replied, but Clara laughed and leaned over, out of sight. "No sense taking any chances, right, Tabitha?"

"Exactly," the older woman said with satisfaction.

Laura steered the car around the house to the back porch, where Josef waited for them. Another man stood beside him, with a large professional camera hanging from his neck.

As soon as Laura stopped, Josef and the young man

hurried forward to help Tabitha and Clara out of the car.

Clara extended her hand to the man. "I'm sorry," she said with a warm smile. "I'm so glad you're here, but I didn't think we'd hired a professional photographer."

"My mother's a guest," he explained. "She works for Kurt and asked me to come take pictures. They'll be her wedding gift to you."

"Oh my gosh," Clara said. "That's so kind of her! I was just saying to Laura a few minutes ago that I wished we'd hired a photographer."

The young man beamed. "I'm here to take a few photos before Josef walks you down the aisle."

"That's perfect," Clara said.

"Ian and I are going to the front porch," Tabitha announced. "We'll see you in a few minutes." She took her grandson's arm, and the two of them headed off.

Josef offered his hand as Clara climbed the few steps to the back porch. "You look radiant, my dear," he said.

Clara smiled up at him. "I can't tell you how much it means that you're walking me down the aisle. Especially under the circumstances. I understand that you and Maisie may have mixed feelings about this."

"Not at all, my dear," Josef said kindly. "In fact, I have something for you from Maisie." He reached into the breast pocket of his jacket and pulled out a delicate handkerchief embroidered with tiny forget-me-nots.

"Maisie's great-grandmother gave this to her on her sixteenth birthday. She'd like you to have it—and to carry it with you as something old."

Clara traced the fine embroidery with trembling fingers. "This is exquisite," she said, her voice catching. "I'm honored."

Laura stood nearby, dabbing at her eyes. "This is such an emotional day," she said with a watery laugh. "I just hope I can make it down the aisle before I start bawling."

"We can't have that!" the young man said cheerfully. "We need beautiful smiles, not red noses, in these photos. Everyone's anxiously waiting for the bride's big entrance—so let's take these pictures and get this party started."

JOSEF HANDED Clara her simple bouquet of calla lilies and baby's breath, tied with a purple satin ribbon. He offered his arm, and Clara slipped her hand through it, steadying herself as they waited for the cue to begin.

From the front of the cottage came the low hum of voices, punctuated by laughter. Everyone fell silent as the opening strains of the evocative "A Thousand Years," covered by The Piano Guys, filled the air.

"Ready?" Josef asked when they heard the first repetition of the famous lyric that preceded the chorus.

Clara nodded. "Ready."

They walked through the house and paused in the open doorway. The small group of friends and family rose from white folding chairs and turned to face her. Kurt stood tall and handsome at one end of the porch, his gaze fixed on her the moment she appeared.

A hush fell over the guests. Even the breeze seemed to still.

Clara's heart thudded in her chest as she met Kurt's eyes. Every flutter of nerves vanished. There was only him—the man who loved her completely, and stood before her now with tears glinting in his eyes.

Josef turned to her and whispered. "You're in good hands now, my dear."

She looked up at him, her throat tight with emotion. "Thank you for everything."

They walked to Kurt as the music swelled. Josef placed Clara's hand gently in Kurt's. "Take good care of each other," he said.

The judge smiled, telling everyone to be seated. "Dearly beloved," he began, "we are gathered here today to celebrate the union of two people who have found in each other their truest companion and closest friend."

Clara felt Kurt's thumb brush over her knuckles, grounding her.

As the ceremony unfolded, she barely heard the words, perceiving only the warmth of Kurt's hand, the soft rustle of falling leaves, and the feeling that everything in her life had led her here, to this perfect moment.

The judge led them through the time-honored vows. "By the power vested in me, I now pronounce you husband and wife. Kurt, you may kiss your bride."

Kurt cupped her face and kissed Clara gently—sweetly—and the guests erupted into applause.

Joan tapped her phone for a second time, and an acoustic version of Shania Twain's "From this Moment On" poured through the connected speakers.

The newlyweds clasped hands and walked to the other end of the porch.

Maisie dabbed her eyes. "Oh, my," she whispered to Tabitha. "That was perfect."

"It most certainly was," replied her dear friend.

CHAPTER 12

Clara pulled the down-filled duvet up to her nose and tucked her knees to her chest. The cottage was much chillier this morning than it had been the night before. Things between her and Kurt had been anything but cold. She smiled to herself and reached out a hand toward him.

The covers on his side of the bed had been thrown back. He wasn't there.

She opened her eyes. The light peeking through the gap in the draperies was almost neon white. It must be close to noon, she thought. Rolling to her other side, she reluctantly snaked a hand out from under the covers to grab her phone from the nightstand. Ten o'clock. Morning still—but so bright. The sun wouldn't yet be on this side of the house.

She pushed up onto her elbows and listened. The

sound of the back door opening and closing reached her, followed by Kurt's footsteps crossing the kitchen and heading toward the living room.

Clara got out of bed and reached for the silk robe lying at the foot of the bed. The room was even colder than she'd imagined, and she quickly abandoned the idea of wrapping herself in the beautiful but flimsy fabric. Instead, she pulled the duvet from the bed and held it close around her as she searched for the sneakers she'd brought for the hike they'd planned later that day.

The duvet trailed behind her like a train as she inched down the stairs. She stepped off the bottom step and into the living room.

Kurt stood at the fireplace, his back to her, busying himself with building a fire.

"Good morning," she said. "What a wonderful idea! You are the best husband."

He glanced over his shoulder and smiled. "Good morning to you, too, Sleeping Beauty." He struck a match, lit the newspaper and kindling, and, before long, the flames caught. "It'll warm up in a few minutes."

"What about the heater?" she asked.

"Good question," he said. "It was working last night, but something's wrong. I can't get it to start. I'll call someone about it tomorrow."

Clara moved closer to the fire, holding out her hands to the heat. "Didn't you tell me your grandparents used to heat the entire house with this fireplace—unless the temperatures plummeted?"

"That's true," he said.

"Then we'll be fine. It's not winter yet, anyway."

"You haven't looked outside this morning, have you?" he asked.

Her eyes widened. She shuffled to the window, pulled back the drape—and gasped. Outside was a flawless blanket of white, unblemished and sparkling in the sunlight as far as the eye could see.

"Oh my gosh," she breathed.

Kurt came to stand behind her, wrapping his arms around her waist. "It is pretty, isn't it?"

"Beyond," she said. "So calm and peaceful. I couldn't have wished for anything more beautiful for the first day of our marriage."

She turned in his embrace, and they kissed for a long time.

"I think that hike's off the list for today," he murmured when they finally broke apart. "We'll have to find something else to do," he teased, tugging playfully at the duvet around her shoulders.

"I'm famished," she said. "I barely ate at our wedding lunch, and somehow we skipped dinner."

"I'm hungry, too," he admitted.

They moved into the kitchen.

"I'm not exactly dressed for cooking," she said,

glancing down at the duvet she clutched.

"Did you pack warm clothes?" he asked.

"Not warm enough," she said with a laugh.

"I've got a flannel shirt and a sweatshirt you can borrow," he offered. "I'll go upstairs and get them for you."

"And my jeans," she called after him. "They're in my suitcase."

"I'll be right back," he said from the stairs. "Just to warn you—there's nothing sexier than a woman in a man's clothes."

"Duly noted," she said, smiling.

Kurt took the stairs two at a time and returned a few minutes later with the requested garments.

Clara got dressed and began cracking eggs while Kurt started the coffee. He pulled a package of bacon from the refrigerator and laid slices in the skillet.

"Where did that come from?" she asked.

"You weren't the only one who thought about provisions for the weekend," he said, grinning.

She leaned in and kissed his cheek.

They worked companionably in the kitchen until breakfast was ready, then filled their plates. They carried their food, the box of pastries, and steaming mugs of coffee to the sofa in front of the fireplace.

Their conversation meandered easily as they relived

the happy moments of the day before, each sharing memories with the other.

"Did you see Laura and Brad together?" Clara asked.

"There were only a handful of guests," Kurt replied. "Of course I saw Laura and Brad."

"No, I mean see them *together*," she said. "They were completely focused on each other. It was like no one else existed."

He smiled. "What are you saying?"

"I think those two made a genuine connection. I saw sparks fly all over the place." She sipped her coffee, raising her eyebrows over the rim of her mug. "I can't believe you didn't notice."

"Well," he said, chuckling, "now that you mention it, they were pretty chummy."

"You think?" she teased. "Are you going to ask him about it?" She set her mug on the coffee table and leaned toward him, eyes bright.

"I won't see him until Thursday," Kurt said. "Why don't you ask Laura?"

"She's flying to Chicago tomorrow, remember? She isn't back until Saturday."

"That's right," Kurt said. "We're staying at your place in town this week—I just didn't remember why."

"Soooo," she said, drawing out the word playfully, "it's up to you to find out what's going on. You need to talk to Brad tomorrow."

"Honey," he said, laughing, "guys don't do that kind of stuff. We don't run around asking, 'Did you like her? Did she like you?' That's what you gals do."

She stared at him.

"Okay, okay," he said, drawing a deep breath. "I'll talk to him."

Clara clasped her hands together and brought them to her chest. "Thank you! Tomorrow, when we get back."

He rolled his eyes, amused. "Will that make you happy?"

She nodded vigorously.

"Then," he said with a grin, "I'll call Brad tomorrow."

CHAPTER 13

Tabitha placed her mug of tea on the kitchen counter and answered the phone on the wall extension. A familiar voice greeted her. "I'm calling from Pinewood Bank. Is this Tabitha Trent?"

"This is she speaking," Tabitha replied. "Is that you, Catherine?"

"Yes—yes, it is!" The voice was warm and enthusiastic. "I'm so glad you recognized me."

"Of course I would, dear. We've known each other for years. How can I help you?"

"Well, I'm calling on a matter of some urgency," Catherine said.

"Oh my," Tabitha replied, concern creeping into her tone.

"I'm calling to confirm that you made a large online transfer from your account," the woman said.

Tabitha pressed the receiver tighter against her ear and reached for the counter to steady herself. "No," she said sharply. "I certainly have not."

The line went silent for a beat. Then the woman spoke again, her tone serious. "Then I'm glad I called. It appears someone is trying to access your account."

"Oh no!" Tabitha cried. "I can't get down to the bank. Laura's out of town until the end of the week, and I don't drive."

"No worries, Mrs. Trent," the woman said soothingly. "I'll put a stop to it right now and freeze your account. Can you give me your login details so I can handle this?"

"Oh yes," Tabitha said. "Laura wrote those down for me. I know exactly where they are."

"Terrific," the woman said. "I'm ready when you are."

"Well, I'm not in the same room with them," Tabitha said. "And it'll take me a few minutes to retrieve them. I don't move as quickly as I used to. But I'll get them and call you right back. I have your direct number—Laura wrote it down for me, too."

"Oh no, please don't hang up," the woman said quickly. "We need to act fast. I'll wait on the line. Take your time."

"That's very kind of you, dear," Tabitha said. "I'm just going to set the receiver down for a moment." She walked into the parlor and opened the little drawer in her end table. Inside were slips of paper with her username, password, and a list of contact numbers for people at the bank.

She hurried back to the kitchen and breathed a sigh of relief when she found the woman still on the line. Tabitha read the username and password carefully, repeating each twice. "I use the same username and password for all my accounts at Pinewood Bank," she added helpfully.

"That's great," the woman said. "Stay on the line just a moment while I confirm that I've gotten into your accounts. I'll put you on a brief hold."

Tabitha waited, her anxiety mounting, until the woman's voice returned.

"We got there just in time, Mrs. Trent. I was able to get into your account, and everything's fine."

"My money's still there?" Tabitha asked, her voice trembling.

"Yes," the woman assured her.

"Oh, Catherine," Tabitha said with heartfelt relief. "I can't thank you enough for looking out for me. One hears such awful stories about people getting scammed online—older folks losing their life savings. It's terrifying. That's why I always come into the bank to do my business."

"You're very wise, Mrs. Trent," the woman said. "Now, I must go. Have a pleasant afternoon."

Tabitha replaced the receiver on its cradle. Then she made herself a fresh cup of tea and carried it into the parlor, sending up a prayer of thanks for Catherine's help.

Clara stood at the window, gazing out at the lawn that stretched from the porch to the tree line. By midafternoon, the snow from the day before had melted, except for a few shady patches beneath the trees. The sun blazed in a cloudless sky.

The kitchen door opened and shut, breaking the silence.

"Everything's loaded," Kurt called as he crossed the kitchen. "Are you ready?"

Clara turned her head over her shoulder but stayed rooted to the spot. "In a minute," she murmured.

"What are you doing?" He came up behind her and wrapped his arms around her.

"I'm taking in the beauty of this place," she replied, "and feeling happier than I've ever been."

Kurt rested his chin on the top of her head. "It's magical," he said. "So calm and peaceful."

She nodded. "Part of me wishes we could shut out the world and stay put."

"I know," he said. "We should definitely come out here as often as possible."

"I'm afraid it's going to be a while," Clara admitted. "November and December are make-or-break months for Sweets & Treats. I'll be working nonstop. But your workload slows down during the holidays—there's no reason you can't visit and enjoy some solitude."

He smiled. "Without you? Not a chance. Besides, I think I'm going to be very busy."

She raised an eyebrow. "Really?"

"I've got a meeting first thing tomorrow morning with a client our firm's been courting for the last year."

"That's exciting. Congratulations!" she said, tilting her head. "Did I know about that before the wedding?"

He shook his head. "I just found out a few minutes ago. I know we said we wouldn't check messages or email, but I took a quick peek while you were getting ready this morning. My assistant put it on my calendar." He gave her a sheepish grin. "Am I forgiven?"

"Of course," she said with a laugh. "In that case, we'd better get going." She turned back to the window and drew the curtains closed.

They clasped hands and walked through the cottage

and out the back door together. As they stepped off the porch and onto the gravel drive, Clara turned back. She kissed her fingertips and touched them to the newel post of the railing.

"We'll be back soon, Bloom Cottage," she whispered.

They continued to hold hands during the short drive back into Pinewood. When the first highway sign for the Pinewood exit appeared, Kurt glanced at her. "Do you mind if we stop at my house to pick up a suit and tie for tomorrow? I don't usually dress that formally, but I need to 'suit up' for this meeting."

"Good idea," Clara said. "We're in no rush. Since we're spending the week at my place, do you want to grab a few more clothes?"

"That'd be great, if you don't mind."

They stopped at his house, and Kurt ferried a week's worth of business and casual clothes to the SUV in a matter of minutes. They continued on their way and turned onto Clara's street before four. Once home, they began carrying in their things. Kurt headed toward her bedroom, and Clara hurried after him.

"My closet's packed," she said. "Let me move some of my stuff to the other bedroom closet so you have room."

He halted. "You don't need to bother. I'll put my clothes in the spare room closet. We'll find a new place soon, so there's no need to go to all that trouble."

"Are you sure?" she asked.

"Positive."

"I'll help you carry the rest of your things in," she said, "and then I want to bring Noelle home."

"You missed her, didn't you?"

"I most certainly did," Clara said. "For someone who's never had a dog, I'm completely attached to her."

"Go on," he said, leaning in to kiss her cheek. "Get your little girl. I'll finish up here."

Clara smiled. "You're the best. We'll be right back."

"Take your time," Kurt said.

"There's an electrical outlet behind your nightstand," Clara added as she headed for the door. "I put a power strip there if you need to plug in your chargers."

"Thank you, sweetheart."

She jogged across the lawn to the main house and sprinted up the steps. Noelle's excited yipping told her the pup knew her mistress was home. Clara opened the back door, and Noelle launched herself into her arms. Clara sat on the step, laughing as the squirming dog covered her chin with kisses.

Ian stepped out the door, holding a plastic milk crate filled with covered aluminum pans. "You're back," he said. "I was bringing this to the guesthouse."

Clara released Noelle and stood. "What's all that?"

"Josef stopped by a few minutes ago—you just missed him. Maisie made dinner for Gran and me, and for you and Kurt."

"Oh my gosh," Clara said. "Those two are so kind."

Ian grinned. "It's rigatoni, a green salad, and bread-sticks. Plus a batch of snickerdoodles."

"Sounds delicious," Clara said. "Did your mom leave this morning as planned?"

He nodded. "She already texted that she's checked into her hotel."

"And everything's been okay here today?"

"Sure," Ian said.

"If anything comes up while your mom's out of town, you can come to Kurt or me—day or night."

"That's what Mom said," Ian replied, straightening his shoulders. "But we'll be fine. I'm not a baby anymore, you know."

"Of course not," Clara said quickly. "You're a very capable young man. No one thinks otherwise." She cleared her throat and extended her hands. "I'll take the food to the cottage."

"I don't mind carrying it," Ian said. "Besides, Gran wants to see you."

"I'd love to say hello," Clara said.

"She's in the parlor."

Ian set off toward the guesthouse. Noelle looked from Ian to Clara.

"Go with Ian," Clara said. "I'll be home in a few minutes."

Noelle wagged her tail once, then bounded off the porch after the teenager.

Tabitha sat in her chair by the bay window, pen poised over the crossword. She looked up as Clara entered. "Clara!" she cried.

"How are you, Tabitha?" Clara asked warmly.

"Couldn't be better," Tabitha said. "I wanted to tell you how much I enjoyed your wedding. It was lovely—and it meant so much to me that you wore my sister's dress. You were an absolute vision."

"That's very kind of you," Clara said. "It was a beautiful day—one Kurt and I will never forget. Thank you for being such an important part of it."

Tabitha set the paper and pen on the end table. "I've been so busy yesterday and today that I haven't even finished Sunday's crossword," she said, pointing to the chair opposite her. "Will you sit a moment? I have news."

Clara sat on the edge of the chair, hoping they wouldn't talk for hours. She was eager to get back to Kurt.

"I won't keep you," Tabitha said, as though reading Clara's mind. "I wanted to ask if you noticed that Laura and Kurt's friend, Brad, took quite a shine to each other at the wedding."

Clara leaned forward, resting her elbows on her knees. "I did," she said. "That's exactly what I told Kurt.

He promised he'd call Brad to find out what was going on."

"Well, you can tell that husband of yours there's no need," Tabitha said, smiling with delight. "Those two have been texting back and forth since Sunday—and he called her, too! He even invited her to dinner that night."

Clara's face broke into a smile.

"But she turned him down," Tabitha added.

Clara's smile faltered.

"Only because she had an early flight Monday morning," Tabitha added quickly.

"That makes sense," Clara said. "So, did they set another date?"

"They most certainly did," Tabitha said, her eyes bright. "Laura gets back Saturday afternoon, and they're going to brunch on Sunday."

Clara clasped her hands together. "Oh, that's such terrific news. I love that!"

"I do too," Tabitha said, nodding. "I was hoping there'd be a single man at your wedding who would be right for Laura."

"I remember you saying that," Clara said with a laugh. "I almost told you about Brad, but I thought we should just wait and see."

Tabitha cocked her head. "I don't believe in coincidences," she said. "I think their meeting was meant to be."

"You may be right." Clara rose and stepped closer, leaning down to kiss her cheek. "I'd better get back to that husband of mine."

"Things seem to be going very well for all of us," Tabitha said, smiling up at her.

Clara grinned. "They certainly do."

CLARA RETURNED TO THE GUESTHOUSE, but Kurt and Ian were nowhere to be seen. She passed through the kitchen toward the back door, expecting to find them outside.

Noelle paced anxiously at the entry to the small laundry room.

"What's going on, girl?" Clara asked.

She stepped into the doorway and stopped short. A rough wooden stairway had been pulled down from the ceiling. Muffled voices drifted from above. *The guesthouse has an attic?*

Clara positioned herself at the base of the steps and carefully climbed until her head and shoulders poked through the opening into an unfinished space.

Kurt and Ian stood in the middle of the attic, balancing on exposed two-by-fours. The ceiling sloped on both sides, but a wide swath down the center afforded full standing height.

"What in the world are you two doing?" she asked.

They spun to face her.

"Did you know there was an attic up here?" Kurt asked.

"No," she admitted. "Although I noticed two small windows along the back wall—you can see them from the yard. I never realized there were pull-down stairs."

"I haven't been up here before," Ian said, eyes wide. "This is so cool!"

"It's a really good space," Kurt said, surveying the room. "I think the bathroom downstairs is right below that spot." He pointed toward one side. "If you extended the pipes, you could add a bathroom up here. If that's too pricey, you could still insulate the roof and walls, install drywall, run electrical, and lay flooring to make this usable."

"That'd be neat," Ian agreed.

"This could be a three-bedroom house," Kurt added. "Maybe even three bedrooms and two baths."

"I think the stairs would be a problem," Clara said thoughtfully. "The laundry room's too small to make them permanent."

"A spiral staircase somewhere else in the house might work," Kurt suggested, his brow furrowed as he visualized it.

Clara laughed. "I can't leave you two alone for a minute, can I?"

Kurt grinned. "Just inspecting my new home."

"It's not his fault," Ian said quickly. "He asked me about that rope coming out of the ceiling, and I said I didn't know—but I wanted to see what it was."

Clara smiled. "So you had to find out. I understand completely."

"Well," Kurt said, glancing around one last time, "now we know. Let's be careful getting out of here," he said to Ian. "If you step off these two-by-fours, you'll go straight through the ceiling."

Clara backed down the stairs, and Kurt and Ian followed.

"Thanks again, Kurt," Ian said once they reached the main floor.

"That was fun," Kurt said.

"I can't wait to tell Mom what we found when she calls tonight."

"It's always good to know the bones of your own home," Kurt said, smiling.

IAN RAN across the lawn and burst through the back door.

Tabitha was standing in the kitchen by the wall phone, rummaging through a small pile of papers on the counter beneath it.

"Hi, Gran," he said. "Can I help you find something?"

Tabitha clutched two slips of paper. "No, thank you, dear. I found what I needed." She looked at him, eyes twinkling. "Your face is flushed—you look like you've got something to say."

"I sure do!" Ian grinned. "Kurt and I found an attic in the guest house. Did you know it even had one?"

"Ahhh …" Tabitha said, nodding slowly. "I did. It's been years since I thought about it."

"Kurt has some really cool ideas about what we could do with that space," Ian said eagerly.

"I'd love to hear all about it," Tabitha replied. "But first let me put these papers away in the drawer by my chair. I shouldn't have left them lying out this afternoon." She reached for her cane and turned toward the parlor. "Are you hungry?"

"Yep! Josef dropped off dinner that Maisie made for you and me."

Tabitha smiled. "She told me she was going to do that."

"I'll put those papers away for you," Ian offered. "Go sit in the dining room, and I'll bring our dinner in there."

"Thank you, dear," Tabitha said. "Be sure to put them in the back of the drawer, under everything else. They're bank papers and need to be stored away safely."

Ian did as she asked, sliding the papers into the

bottom of the drawer. They soon sat at the dining table, chatting freely as they enjoyed Maisie's delicious meal.

CHAPTER 15

*L*aura drained the last drops of her vanilla almond latte and set the oversized cup back on its saucer. She dabbed her lips with the linen napkin and arranged it in her lap.

"This is the best meal I've had in a long time," she said, smiling across the table at Brad.

"Briarwood Kitchen just opened a couple of months ago," Brad said. "My construction company helped renovate this old barn and turn it into the farm-to-table restaurant we're sitting in now."

"It's beyond charming," Laura said, running her fingertips along the antique tabletop, its grain burnished to a honey-gold glow by decades of shared meals. "I love that every table and chair is different. The canning jar centerpieces full of dried flowers are the only things that match."

Brad followed her gaze. "The owner did the interior design herself. She's got a great eye. I hear Pam plans to open a little antiques shop in one of the outbuildings next spring."

"I love that idea," Laura said. "Clara and I will come for lunch and a bit of shopping. Will you do the renovation?"

"Definitely," Brad said, his smile easy. "I'll always say yes to a job for Pam. Once the kitchen was finished and we were working on the interior, she started making breakfast for my crew every morning—said we were her taste testers."

Laura laughed. "That must have been wonderful! If everything else is as good as these eggs Benedict, I bet your crew loved her."

"They did," Brad said, chuckling. "I teased her that if she kept feeding us like that, we'd never finish the job. Nobody wanted the project to end."

"Who could blame them?" Laura said. "I'm glad you brought me here. I'll bet that in another six months the line will be out the door."

"I think so, too," Brad said. "I hope it is—for her sake. Pam's a single mom and runs this place with her sister, Paula. Both of them work hard and deserve to be successful."

Laura looked out the wide barn windows at the view beyond. Fields rolled gently toward the horizon. "It's a beautiful setting. Perfect to sit outside when the weather warms up."

"She's already talked to me about building an outdoor patio in the spring," Brad said.

Laura smiled. "These hills remind me of the area around Bloom Cottage."

"Clara and Kurt's place is about twenty miles southeast of here," Brad said. "This whole ridge runs the same line."

"I haven't been in the country for years," Laura admitted. "Between teaching and taking care of Gran and Ian, I never seem to have the time. But I think my mom used to bring us out here every fall to buy apples. I remember a huge fruit stand with rows and rows of baskets, each full of a different variety of apple. She was a wonderful baker and extremely particular about the varieties to use for sauce or pies, and which were best for eating. If I behaved, she'd let me get a caramel apple to take home."

Brad smiled. "Let me guess. You always got a caramel apple, didn't you?"

Laura laughed. "Either I was a very well-behaved child, or my mom was kind and generous."

"Maybe both," he said, his eyes warm.

"I wonder whatever happened to that place," Laura mused.

"These back roads are full of old farm stands," Brad

said. "We might not find the exact one you remember, but, if we take the long way home instead of the highway, I'm sure we'll come across one or two. What do you say?"

"Oh, I'd love that!" Laura cried. "It would be wonderful to bring home freshly picked apples from an orchard instead of in a plastic bag from the grocery store. Are you sure you have time?"

Brad smiled and leaned in slightly. "There's nothing I'd rather do than spend the afternoon with you."

Laura's cheeks flushed pink.

Brad paid the check, and they stepped out into the crisp autumn air. He took her hand in his as they headed toward his truck—two smiling figures setting off for whatever surprises the afternoon might hold.

THE COUNTRY ROAD curved lazily through rolling hills, sunlight flickering through a canopy of golden leaves.

Laura gazed out the windshield, her hair catching the light as they sped along. "This feels like stepping back in time," she said.

Brad smiled. "That's what I love about these roads—no billboards, no traffic lights. Just farms, trees, and the occasional tractor."

They drove in companionable silence for a few miles

until Laura spotted a faded red sign painted with cheerful letters: Duncan's Orchard—Fresh Apples, Cider, and Pies.

"There!" she said, pointing. "I'll bet that's just like the place my mom used to bring us."

Brad slowed and turned off the road. They followed the lane another half mile, passing rows of apple trees aligned in perfect symmetry, stretching to the horizon. Another weathered red sign, with an arrow pointing left and Duncan's painted beneath it, guided their way.

Brad turned, the truck's tires crunching over gravel as they wove past rows of parked cars, searching for a parking space. The old fruit stand stood at the far end of the parking lot, a wooden sign proclaiming Best Apple Pie in the Midwest! swinging gently in the breeze.

Laura jumped out as soon as they parked, her eyes gleaming with excitement. "Oh, Brad," she said, "this is exactly as I remember."

They walked toward the fruit stand and joined the back of one of four long lines.

"I'm a terrible line-picker," Laura said with a laugh. "No matter which one I choose, it's always the slowest."

"We're in no rush," Brad replied. "Ten minutes more or less won't change a thing." He smiled, watching her take it all in—the baskets brimming with apples, the scent of cinnamon and sugar drifting from a nearby pie case, and the faint hum of country music playing on the radio.

Behind the counter, a silver-haired woman in a red flannel shirt greeted them warmly. "Afternoon, folks! Picking or buying?"

"Buying," Laura said with a smile. "But I might have to pick one—just to say I did."

"Go right ahead," the woman said, nodding toward the orchard. "We let every customer pick one apple on the house. You can pay for your order now, and we'll place it in the holding area for pickup. That way, you won't have to wait in line again unless you get carried away."

"That's helpful," Laura said.

"What'll you have today?" the woman asked, fingers poised over the keys of an old-fashioned cash register.

"A bushel of Pink Ladies for applesauce," Laura said, "and one of Honeycrisps for pies."

"Excellent choices," the woman said, ringing up the order.

Laura reached for her wallet, but Brad handed cash across the counter.

"You're not paying for my apples," Laura protested.

"I have ulterior motives," he said with a grin. "When I heard you mention apple pies, I was hoping I might be invited over for a slice."

Laura laughed. "With a whole bushel of apples, I'll

make you your own pie—and, if you like applesauce, you'll have some of that, too."

The woman tied numbered tags to the baskets and called to a teenage boy, who carried them to the holding area. She handed Brad a receipt. "Honeycrisps are the sweetest this week," she said, gesturing toward the orchard. "Each row is marked with the variety."

Laura and Brad thanked her and stepped out of the line. They wandered between the trees, the ground soft with fallen leaves and the air crisp and fragrant.

Brad found the Honeycrisp section and reached up to pluck a rosy apple from a low branch. He polished it on his sleeve and held it out to Laura.

She took a bite. "Oh," she sighed, "that's delicious."

Brad grinned. "Let me try."

She held the apple out to him, and, when he leaned in for a bite, their hands brushed. For a heartbeat, neither moved.

Brad took a bite.

Laura lowered the apple, her cheeks flushed. "So?"

"Sweet," Brad replied. "That lady was right."

They returned to the stand and collected their two bushels of apples.

"Are you sure you can carry that?" Brad asked. "I'll take one to the truck and come back for the other."

Laura rolled her eyes, smiling. "I can handle a bushel of apples, thank you very much."

They walked slowly to his parking spot, the sun dipping low behind the trees and casting long amber shadows in front of them.

Laura glanced at Brad. "This might be one of the best days I've had in years."

"Then let's make sure it's not the last one like it," Brad said.

She smiled, her heart skipping a beat.

The truck doors shut, gravel crunched beneath the tires, and they pulled away from Duncan's Orchard—leaving behind the scent of apples, the golden light of late afternoon, and the promise of something beautiful just beginning.

CHAPTER 16

*L*ater that evening, after Tabitha had retired and Ian had gone to his room, Laura curled up on the sofa in the parlor, wrapped in her plush robe. A candle on the coffee table filled the room with the scent of apples and vanilla.

Laura smiled to herself as she scrolled through the photos on her phone—rows of apple trees glowing in the late-day sun, Brad smiling with a half-eaten apple in his hand, and the rolling hills looking like they could be in a landscape painting.

Her phone buzzed with an incoming call from Clara. Laura answered quickly. "Hi. How're things going for my favorite newlyweds?"

Clara's cheerful voice came through the line. "Wonderful. But enough about me. I want to hear about your brunch date."

Laura giggled. "It wasn't only brunch—it turned into an entire day. Brad took me to this amazing farm-to-table restaurant he renovated, and afterward we went apple picking."

"Apple picking?" Clara echoed, her tone teasing. "That sounds awfully romantic. Next you'll tell me he carried your apples to the truck and gazed into your eyes over a cider doughnut."

"You're half right," Laura said, grinning, "He carried my apples. And yes, there might have been some gazing involved."

Clara squealed. "Oh, Laura, that's wonderful! I had a feeling about you two from the wedding."

Laura leaned her head back on the sofa cushion, smiling at the ceiling. "He's so easy to be with. Funny. Kind. And he listens—really listens. It's been a long time since I felt so … at ease with someone."

"You deserve that. After everything you've done for Tabitha and Ian, and everyone else, it's your turn to have some joy."

Laura hesitated, her voice guarded. "It's only one date, Clara. I don't want to get ahead of myself."

"Who said anything about getting ahead?" Clara teased. "Just enjoy it. Sometimes the best things happen when you're not planning them."

"I know," Laura said. "And you're right. Today felt like … a beginning."

"Good," Clara said. "Because I have a feeling Brad isn't the kind of man who lets something good slip away."

Laura sighed. "I should let you go," she said. "Tell Kurt I said hello."

"You've got it," Clara said. "And Laura?"

"Hmm?"

"I'm really happy for you."

Laura's throat tightened a little. "Thanks. That means a lot."

They said their goodnights, and, when the call ended, Laura set her phone aside and let the quiet settle around her.

She didn't know what might come next, but, for the first time in a long time, the uncertainty felt like hope.

THE NEXT MORNING, Brad parked his truck at a construction site on the edge of Pinewood, coffee steaming in his insulated mug. The crisp November air smelled of raw earth and new lumber. His crew was already unloading supplies, the clatter of boards and hum of power tools filling the air.

He sipped his coffee, but his thoughts weren't on blueprints or timelines. They were on Laura. He could picture her perfectly: standing beneath a branch heavy with apples, her cheeks flushed and her eyes bright with that spark of humor and kindness that had drawn him in from the start.

He smiled, shaking his head at himself. He'd gone on plenty of dates before, but none that lingered quite like this. Something about Laura felt different—real, genuine.

His phone buzzed, and the screen told him it was Kurt. He answered the call, and, before he could utter a greeting, Kurt asked, "Good weekend?"

Brad hesitated, then chuckled. "Yeah. Really good, actually."

"I need more than that, bro. Clara's been hounding me since last night to find out how your date with Laura went."

"Let's just say I may have had the best day of my life."

"Whoa. That's really something, coming from you. You've always been super cautious before falling for someone."

"Let's keep it between ourselves. I think she likes me, but it's too soon to tell."

"She likes you. Clara called her last night. She's smitten, too."

Brad remained silent, savoring the news.

"Brad?"

"I'm here," he replied. "Don't you have to be in court or something?"

"As a matter of fact, I do. I'll let you go."

"Okay."

"And Brad, I'm really happy for you, man."

They disconnected the call.

Brad turned back toward the job site, but his mind was stuck on Laura as if in a perpetual loop. Her slightly lopsided smile, those intelligent eyes, and the way she focused on him when he was talking—like he was the most interesting person in the room—stirred something in him. He'd told her they should make sure there were more days like yesterday, and he'd meant it.

His phone buzzed again, and his pulse quickened when he checked the screen. A text from Laura.

Thank you again for yesterday. I can't stop smiling.

He felt his chest tighten in the best way. He typed back before he could overthink it.

Me too. How about dinner this weekend?

Her reply came almost instantly.

Absolutely. I can't wait.

Brad smiled and tucked the phone into his pocket. Now, all he had to do was get through the next five days before seeing her again.

CHAPTER 17

*C*lara retrieved her raincoat from the coat rack in the workroom and slung her purse over her shoulder.

Joan looked up from the batch of croissants she was placing on baking sheets for their second rise. "You're going out in this weather?"

"Not for a walk," Clara replied, fastening her coat. "I have an errand to run, so I'll drive."

For the past week and a half, Clara had walked the residential neighborhoods around the downtown square every afternoon, looking for For Sale signs during the lull between lunch and the after-school rush. They'd hired Kurt's realtor friend to keep an eye out, too, and Kurt checked online listings twice a day. Still, it never hurt to have boots on the ground.

"I'll be back in half an hour," she said.

"We're in good shape," Joan replied. "Don't worry if it takes longer."

Clara nodded, pulled the hood of her raincoat over her head, and dashed to her SUV. She backed out of the alley behind Sweets & Treats and covered the familiar streets from her daily walks in half the time. She checked the clock on her dashboard. She had time to widen her search and still be back before the shop got busy.

The neighborhoods surrounding the square stretched for half a mile in every direction—streets lined with mature oaks and maples, their branches arching overhead. Some homes were grand, like Tabitha's red-brick Victorian, while others were modest Craftsman cottages like Maisie and Josef's. Each was unique, sitting proudly on wide, tree-lined lots with generous side-walks separated from the street by tidy tree lawns. The charm of the neighborhood was undeniable.

This is where I want to put down roots, Clara thought. *Here, with Kurt. This is where we'll raise our family.*

She completed a third loop around the square and had started a fourth when something caught her eye—a small white rectangle fixed to a front porch railing. She slowed to a crawl, wipers slapping furiously across the windshield. Squinting through the rain-blurred glass, she slammed on the brakes when she could finally read the words:

FOR SALE BY OWNER.

Clara pulled into an opening at the curb two houses down, grabbed her umbrella from the driver's side door pocket, and launched herself into the storm. The wind shoved against her umbrella as she bent her head and trudged toward the house.

Rain spattered across her face as she reached the house and stopped. Despite the weather, the sight of the home made her heart lift.

It was a red-brick beauty—old, but solid, with character in every line. A generous front porch wrapped around both sides, vanishing from view. Identical bay windows graced the center of the first and second floors, and a circular spoked window, like a wagon wheel, adorned the gable above.

It wasn't a replica of Tabitha's Victorian, but it could have been its cousin. *Maybe it was designed by the same architect.* Standing there, drenched to the skin, Clara felt strangely warm just looking at it.

She checked her watch. She should have been back twenty minutes ago, but Joan had said not to rush, hadn't she?

A gust of wind caught Clara's umbrella and wrenched it backward. She stumbled, then planted her feet and fought to close it. She held her coat tightly at the neck and hurried up the walkway toward the front steps.

The narrow porch creaked beneath her shoes. She pushed her hood back and glanced through the beveled glass windows on either side of the front door. No movement. The curtains on the bay window were drawn tight. Upstairs, no light glimmered through the rain.

"I believe you're vacant," Clara muttered.

She pressed the doorbell and waited, rainwater dripping from her coat onto the faded doormat. No answer.

She tried again. Still nothing.

Moving along the porch, she peered through a large side window. Café curtains covered the upper half, and what she could see below was dim and bare. A circular ceramic planter sat along the railing, its contents long since dead.

Clara hesitated, then grasped the heavy pot with both hands. Too heavy to lift, she managed to tilt it onto its rim and roll it beneath the window. Balancing carefully, she planted one foot on the pot's edge. Her heart thudded. "What on earth are you doing?" she muttered. Vacant or not, she shouldn't be snooping.

Just as she lifted her other foot, a sharp gust of wind caught her, knocking her off balance. She flailed for the railing, caught it, and steadied herself, her breath coming fast. "Okay," she whispered, "that's my sign. I shouldn't be doing this."

Still, curiosity won. She climbed onto the pot more

carefully this time. Shielding her face from the rain, she pressed her nose to the glass. Inside was a small kitchen. A stainless-steel sink sat beneath the window, flanked by chipped Formica countertops. A narrow electric stove crouched on the opposite wall, and the spot where a refrigerator once stood gaped empty. The wallpaper hung in curling strips, and the ceiling bore brown water stains.

Clara stepped down, repositioned the planter, and continued around the house. A plain wooden door opened from the rear of the house onto the porch, with steps leading into a backyard gone wild with overgrown shrubs and tangled trees. The leafless limbs afforded a view of a yard that stretched at least three hundred feet —deep and full of potential.

She tested the doorknob. It was locked.

"Just as well," she murmured. "I won't be facing a breaking-and-entering charge today."

The rain showed no sign of letting up. Clara returned to the front of the house and ran down the front steps. She paused at the sidewalk, rainwater dripping from her hair and coat. The house loomed before her, steady and beautiful despite its wear.

If the rest of it's in the same shape as that kitchen, she thought, *this will be the ultimate fixer-upper.* Her gaze followed the line of the porch up to the spoked attic window. Something about it stirred her—the same certainty she'd felt the first time she'd seen Tabitha's home.

"Yes," she whispered to herself. "It's time to call Kurt. We need to tour this house. It might be the one."

KURT ANSWERED on the first ring. "Hey, sweetheart."

"Am I interrupting?" Clara asked, turning up the heater in her car so her teeth would stop chattering.

"You caught me between appointments," he said. "I've got ten minutes."

"Perfect. I think I found it."

"It?"

"Our forever home."

Kurt paused before answering. "Really? I checked the online listings on my lunch break—nothing new came up in the area we want."

"Maybe it's not on the MLS," Clara said. "There's a For Sale by Owner sign zip-tied to the porch railing."

"I see," he said, his tone shifting with interest.

"I took a photo, though it's a little blurry from the rain. I'm texting it to you now." She scrolled to her photos, sent it, and waited. "Well?"

A moment later, she heard the click of his phone. "Ah, I can see why you like it," he said. "That red brick, the big porch, bay windows on both floors—it looks like a smaller version of Tabitha's house."

"Exactly!" Clara said. "What do you think?"

"It's got curb appeal, that's for sure."

"I'm afraid the inside might be a little rough."

He chuckled. "Did you go through it?"

"No. It looks vacant. I rang the bell, but no one answered."

"Maybe they weren't home."

"There's no refrigerator," Clara said—then bit her lip, instantly regretting it.

Kurt laughed. "You said you didn't go inside. How do you know that?"

"Let's just say I may have gotten a little creative with a flowerpot," she admitted.

He groaned. "You didn't—"

"I didn't go inside," she said quickly. "I just … peeked."

"Of course you did. And if I know you, you even tried the door."

"I can neither confirm nor deny, counselor," Clara replied, her voice full of mock innocence.

He laughed. "Well, I think we need to see it properly. I'll call our realtor and have him reach out to the owner. Did you get a photo of the sign? I assume there's a phone number."

"Sending it now," she said, thumbs flying over her screen.

"There's so little inventory," Kurt said. "If we're interested, we need to move fast. If he can get us in tomorrow, I'll clear my calendar. How about you?"

"Same," Clara said. "I'll make myself available."

"I'll drive by on my way home."

"Let's go together after dinner," Clara said. "I want to see your genuine reaction. I need you to love it as much as I do."

"That's very sweet," he said with a smile in his voice, "but I'm not sure I'll ever feel about a house the same way you do."

"Oh, one more thing," Clara said quickly. "It has a huge backyard—for Noelle."

"I was just going to ask," Kurt said, amused.

Clara sneezed loudly.

"Bless you! I hope you didn't catch pneumonia creeping around that property in the rain."

"Nope," she said, sniffing. "Not happening. The heater's blasting, and I'll drink hot tea at the patisserie the rest of the afternoon."

"Okay, my love," Kurt chuckled. "I'll pick up carryout from the diner on my way home. We'll scarf down dinner and go see this mystery house you've found."

"You read my mind," Clara said, smiling. "This is exciting. Shopping for our forever home!"

CHAPTER 18

Kurt and Clara huddled under his umbrella the next day at the rear property line of the house.

Clara drew a deep breath and let out a contented sigh. "That would be the perfect spot for a swing set," she said, pointing to an open patch of lawn on their right.

"I've always wanted to build one of those fancy play structures they have now," Kurt replied, grinning. "You know—the kind with a playhouse, swings, climbing ropes, and slides."

"You could make that?" she asked.

"Piece of cake," he said with mock confidence.

Clara laughed and hugged his arm tighter. "That would be wonderful."

Kurt turned to study the fence behind them, its

boards leaning and splintered. "We'll need to replace this fence first. That Houdini of a dog would find a way out the moment we moved in."

"Good point," Clara said. "We don't want another blizzard escape."

He chuckled. "Everything turned out fine that time, but once was enough. I'll add it to the list of immediate repairs."

"The inside needs plenty of work, too," Clara said, glancing up at him. "What do you think?"

"I'll have Brad take a look to confirm," Kurt said, "but I'm certain it needs to come down to the studs. The roof's shot." He pointed to the sagging gutter at the back. "We'll need new plumbing, sewer lines, and electrical. I expect nothing in this place is up to code."

"That's before we even get to the finishes," Clara said.

He nodded. "The kitchen and both bathrooms will have to be redone completely. And I suggest we add a second bath upstairs. There's plenty of room."

"We'll want that," she agreed. "Especially once the kids come along."

He grinned his agreement. "Then there's flooring, walls, lighting fixtures, doorknobs, hinges—basically everything," Kurt said.

"I love those old glass doorknobs," Clara said wistfully. "Can we keep them?"

"Sure," he said. "It'll just take some elbow grease to clean them up."

She pursed her lips. "Time that neither of us has. We'll have to hire the work out."

"I'm afraid so," Kurt agreed.

"How long do you think it'll take?"

"I'd guess six months to a year. We'll hire Brad's company, so we'll get a fair price and top-notch work."

"Thank goodness we have places to live in the meantime," Clara said.

"These renovations will be expensive," Kurt said.

"I know," Clara replied. "I've got a small reserve set aside for Sweets & Treats, which I'll contribute, but I'm afraid most of the cost will fall to you."

Kurt shook his head. "Hang on to your money. We can always borrow what we need for the renovation, but I think we should sell my house."

"Now?"

He nodded. "I've got plenty of equity in it. That way, we can buy this place without taking on more debt than we need to."

"That means we'd be cramped in the guesthouse for a while," Clara said. "It's a big sacrifice for you. Are you sure?"

Kurt covered her hand with his and gave it a squeeze. "I am. Besides, we don't know how long it'll take my place to sell. It's smart to list it now if we're serious about buying this one."

They stood shoulder to shoulder, gazing up at the back of the home as the rain softened to a mist.

A tall, silver-haired man in a trench coat appeared around the corner of the porch.

Kurt waved. "There's Dan," he said. "Are we in agreement?"

"Yes," Clara said, her voice bubbling with excitement. "Let's tell him we want to make an offer."

They picked their way carefully across the muddy yard and joined their realtor on the back porch.

Dan grinned broadly. "Well, judging by those faces, I'd say you're ready to move forward."

Kurt laughed. "You're a mind reader."

"Not really," Dan said with a wink. "You're hard to read, Kurt, but Clara's eyes are giving you away. She's in love—with this house."

Clara tried to hide her smile, making a mock grimace.

"Let's make sure she never ends up in the same room with the sellers," Kurt said dryly.

Dan chuckled. "Deal. Now, I ran some quick comps on my phone. The asking price is a little high. I'd suggest we come in about twenty thousand under."

"Do you think there'll be a bidding war?" Clara asked.

"If it were in better condition, yes," Dan said. "But this is a major project. A lot of buyers won't want to tackle it."

"What about flippers?" Kurt asked.

"There'll be a few sniffing around," Dan said. "But they won't pay full price."

Kurt looked out across the yard, thinking.

"Are you two sure you're up for a full renovation?" Dan asked. "When we talked last month, you said you wanted something move-in ready."

"That would've been ideal," Kurt said. "But as you pointed out, homes like that in this neighborhood are rare. If we wait for perfect, we might miss our chance. We can make this one our own."

Dan nodded. "A bird in the hand, huh? That's solid thinking."

Kurt turned to Clara. "What do you think?"

She reached out and touched the brick wall. "I can see us living here happily for the rest of our lives."

"Me too." He smiled and turned to Dan. "Let's make a full-price offer. We don't want to lose it, and there's no sense haggling."

Dan's grin widened, bright against the gray sky. "I'll start the paperwork as soon as I'm back at the office."

"Perfect," Kurt said. "We'll stop by around five to sign."

"Sounds good." Dan shook Clara's hand, then Kurt's. "I think you two are making a wise decision."

"Thanks, Dan," Kurt said. "And, as we discussed, please prepare the paperwork to list my place. See you this evening."

The three of them walked along the porch toward the front of the house.

When Dan headed for his car, Clara turned to Kurt, eyes shining.

"There's one more thing I want to do before we go," she whispered.

"Oh?"

She rose onto her toes, cupped his face in her hands, and kissed him.

The rain had almost stopped. A sliver of sunshine sliced through the clouds as they broke apart, both smiling.

"Looks like we just bought ourselves a project," Kurt said.

Clara laughed. "Looks like we just bought ourselves a home."

CHAPTER 19

J oan flipped the Open sign on the door to Closed and switched off the overhead lights in the shop's storefront.

Clara sat at her desk in the workroom, finishing the day's bank deposit. "This is the best weekend we've had in months," she said, leaning back in her chair and tucking an escaped strand of hair into the bun she wore while working.

"I was hoping to hear that," Joan said, walking in and wiping her hands on a towel. "We were slammed both days. And now that you're about to become the proud owner of one of the biggest money pits in Pinewood's history, you'll need every dollar you can get your hands on."

Clara gave her a rueful smile. "The seller still hasn't accepted our offer. It's been four days. I don't know

120

what's taking them so long—we may not get that house after all."

"They haven't turned you down, have they?"

"No," Clara said. "But I can't help feeling there's some kind of problem."

"Maybe they'll come back with a counteroffer."

"Kurt says that's not likely since we offered the full asking price. He won't admit it, but I think he's worried, too."

Joan shook her head. "You're both being silly. You don't know anything for sure yet. I've wasted too much time worrying about things that never happened. My advice? Put it out of your mind until you get your answer."

"Our realtor's going to contact the seller tomorrow if we still haven't heard," Clara said.

"There you go," Joan replied. "Make a plan to be sad on Monday if they turn you down. In the meantime, go home and enjoy the evening with that dreamy husband of yours."

Clara's lips curved into a soft smile at the mention of Kurt. "He is pretty dreamy, I'll admit."

Joan turned in a circle, surveying the spotless work-room. "Everything's cleaned up and put away. I say it's time we blew this pop stand."

Clara rose and picked up the night deposit bag.

"Let me drop that off for you," Joan said. "I drive right by the bank on my way home."

"Thanks," Clara said, handing her the bag. "I hope you know how much I appreciate you."

Joan smiled. "I do."

They stepped out the back door into the crisp late afternoon and headed for their cars.

"See you Tuesday," Clara called.

"Something tells me you'll have good news by then," Joan replied as she walked away.

CLARA STIFLED a yawn as she turned onto her street. She was always tired at the end of a workweek, but the stress of waiting for news on the house had drained her energy more than usual. She wanted nothing more than takeout for dinner, a long soak in the tub, and to curl up next to Kurt.

She smiled when she saw Brad's truck parked along the curb. He and Laura were spending more and more time together.

Pulling past the house, she parked by the garage next to Kurt's SUV. Before her feet hit the payment, Noelle came bounding toward her, tail wagging furiously.

Clara dropped to one knee and gathered the dog in

her arms. "What are you doing out here? You're supposed to be in the backyard, young lady."

Noelle wriggled free and dashed off toward the guesthouse. Clara laughed and rounded the corner of the garage—then froze.

Laura and Tabitha sat in chairs on her front porch, smiling. Brad, Kurt, and Ian were tossing a football on the lawn. Noelle chased after each throw, barking in delight but never quite catching the ball. A bouquet of balloons was tied to the porch railing—one shiny Mylar balloon shaped like a house bobbed above the rest, emblazoned with a single word: Congratulations!

Clara's hand flew to her chest. It must be … *we got the house*!

She let out an exuberant whoop and broke into a run through the grass, straight toward Kurt.

He turned just in time to catch her as she threw herself into his arms, nearly knocking him off balance.

"It's— we—?" she gasped.

He grinned. "Yep. They signed our offer—no changes."

Clara pressed her hands to her temples, beaming. "That's incredible! We'll be homeowners by mid-December!"

Kurt laughed. "Quite a Christmas gift we're giving each other. I'm not sure how we'll ever top this."

"We won't need to," Clara said, her smile radiant.

"There's more," Kurt added. "Another agent in Dan's office has a client extremely interested in my place."

"You're kidding," Clara said. "How did they hear about it?"

"Dan presented my house at their weekly agent's meeting. This buyer is a couple moving here to be close to family. He's a doctor and has taken a position at the hospital. She's seven months pregnant, with twins. They have a toddler and a preschooler. They've been outbid on everything they've tried to buy."

"That's awful! They must be frantic to get settled before the babies come."

"They are. Her mother and sister are going to go through it tomorrow. Dan says that, if they like it, the couple will make an offer—a really good offer. They don't want to risk losing this one. Their backup plan is to move in with her mother. Everyone is eager for them to buy my house."

Clara chuckled. "Everything's falling into place for us. It really is meant to be."

"I think so, too," he said, matching her grin.

Clara nodded toward the porch, where Brad and Ian had joined Laura and Tabitha. "So … everyone knows?"

Kurt chuckled. "Sorry—you weren't the first. I was going to surprise you with the balloons when you got home, but Brad and Laura pulled up just as I was getting them out of my SUV. Since Brad already knew about the renovation estimates, he figured it out immediately."

"Of course he did," Clara said, laughing. "The cat never stood a chance of staying in the bag."

"Then Laura ran to tell Ian and Tabitha. It was almost time for you to get home, and they decided to wait for you together—so they could see your face." Kurt grinned. "Judging by your reaction, I'd say the surprise worked."

Kurt and Clara linked arms and walked toward their friends.

"I know exactly which house you're talking about," Tabitha said warmly. "I absolutely love it—reminds me of this one." She gestured toward her own red-brick Victorian across the lawn.

"That's what we thought, too," Clara said.

Brad extended his hand to Kurt. "Congratulations, man—or maybe condolences. Time will tell."

"With you handling the renovations," Kurt said, shaking his hand, "I'm confident it'll be the former."

Laura stepped forward and hugged Clara. "I'm so happy for you. I wish we could live this close forever, but I know that's not realistic. The guesthouse is too small. Still, I'm thrilled you found your forever home."

"Thank you," Clara said, returning the hug. "But I'm afraid you'll have to put up with us here for a while longer. Brad says the renovations will take six months to a year."

"So you're not moving into Kurt's house?" Laura asked.

Clara shook her head. "Nope. We're selling it right away to help pay for our new—*how had Joan put it?*—our money pit."

Laura laughed. "Well, I hope Brad doesn't work too fast. We love having you here."

"This calls for a celebration," Brad announced. "Kurt and Clara have a new house, and I've got a new renovation project. Dinner's on me."

CHAPTER 20

Josef pulled into the driveway of Kurt's house and parked behind his SUV. Kurt had called after lunch to say that almost everything had sold. The company he'd hired to conduct the moving sale had done an excellent job—only a few items remained, which the crew had packed up to deliver to a donation center.

Josef stepped over the threshold into the now-empty house. He remembered the first time he'd crossed that same doorway years ago, when his daughter and son-in-law had proudly invited him and Maisie to see their first home. Kurt and Rachel had been so excited, their joy filling every corner.

A wave of sadness washed over him. He'd witnessed their journey together—their laughter, their plans, their growing love. Those had been some of the happiest years of his life. Until everything changed. Until Rachel's diagnosis. Her fight. Her loss.

He brushed a hand across his eyes. He'd come to support Kurt today, knowing the man he loved like a son would be wrestling with more than just logistics. Letting go of this house meant letting go of another piece of the past.

"Kurt?" Josef called.

"Up here," came the reply.

Josef climbed the stairs. "I'm glad I caught you," he said as he reached the landing. "I wanted to see if you needed—"

He stopped. Kurt stood in the hallway, a hand swiping at his eyes. "I wasn't expecting ..." Kurt began, his voice rough with emotion.

"I know," Josef said gently, cutting him off. "Me neither. This place is full of memories. It's impossible not to feel them." He walked to Kurt and draped an arm across his shoulders. For a while, they stood in silence, both lost in their own thoughts.

Finally, Kurt spoke. "Knowing a young family is moving in—it's comforting."

Josef nodded. "I think Rachel would've loved that."

They descended the stairs slowly, each step echoing in the empty house.

"The company you hired did a nice job clearing everything away," Josef said.

"They really did," Kurt replied. "I've got a professional cleaning crew coming tomorrow. The new owners are expected to arrive by noon on Tuesday. They'll pick up the keys from the real estate office, and it'll be done."

"I'm glad you mentioned that," Josef said. "Maisie asked me to find out when they're arriving. She and Clara want to drop off a box of pastries and some cookies for the family."

Kurt grinned. "Of course they do. Those two never miss a chance to be kind."

"We married good ones," Josef said, smiling. "I still have a key. Would it be all right if I drop their treats off around nine on Tuesday? I'll put them on the kitchen island and leave my key."

"Perfect," Kurt said. "Thank you, Josef. I'm grateful for the way everything's worked out. Having the sale proceeds in hand will make it a lot easier to start renovations on the new house once we close escrow."

Josef nodded. "You know what they say—what goes around comes around. I'd say you and Clara have pretty fine karma."

Kurt's smile deepened. "Maybe. I just know I feel blessed."

The two men stepped out onto the front porch. Kurt paused, turning back to take one last look inside the home that had once been the center of his world. He pulled the door shut, checked the lock, and followed Josef to their cars.

"I'll see you Tuesday at the diner," Kurt said.

"Are you still coming to help pack the Thanksgiving food boxes?"

"I wouldn't miss it for the world," Kurt replied.

Kurt nodded. "Handing them out on Wednesday—that's one of my favorite days of the year."

"Mine too," Josef said.

They exchanged a quiet wave before climbing into their vehicles. Josef started his car and gave a small, respectful salute as he backed out of the driveway—leaving behind a house full of memories.

CHAPTER 21

Laura intercepted the mail carrier before the woman reached their porch. The carrier handed over a thick stack of envelopes, two of them glossy with foil embossing that looked like Christmas cards. They exchanged cheerful wishes for a Happy Thanksgiving before parting ways.

Laura set the mail on the kitchen counter and crossed into the parlor, where Tabitha sat in her favorite chair, reading.

"You're home early today," Tabitha said, glancing up from her book.

"We only had a half day because Thanksgiving's tomorrow," Laura said, dropping onto the arm of the sofa.

"How nice," Tabitha replied. "And since we're joining Maisie, Josef, Clara, and Kurt at the diner for Thanksgiving, you don't have to fuss in the kitchen. Maybe you can actually relax for a change." She gestured toward her book with a teasing smile.

"I was thinking the same thing," Laura said. "Brad's coming by tomorrow evening for dessert. I'm going to make two apple pies now. One for dessert and one for him to take home. Then I'll take a nap."

"Excellent plan," Tabitha approved. "Naps are always encouraged. Where's Ian? Didn't he get off early, too?"

"He went to a friend's house—he's staying for dinner. So it's just us tonight."

"Then let's keep it simple," Tabitha said. "When you're done with your nap, we'll scramble eggs, make some toast, and call it good."

"That sounds perfect," Laura said.

She went to her room, changed into sweatpants and a cozy sweatshirt, and returned to the kitchen. Moving the pile of mail to one side, she muttered, "I'll deal with you once the pies are in the oven." She reached for her rolling pin, paring knife, and the basket of apples from her orchard trip.

"Will you put on some music?" Tabitha called.

Laura found a gospel station playing hymns of Thanksgiving and turned up the volume. The house filled with the scent of apples and cinnamon as she worked—cutting shortening into flour, rolling dough into neat circles, and slicing fragrant apples for the filling. She crimped the crusts into delicate scallops and added tiny apple-shaped cutouts from the dough scraps.

When the pies went into the oven, Laura cleaned up the counter, poured herself a cup of coffee, and sat down at the kitchen table with the stack of mail. She opened the Christmas cards first, admiring the artwork and lingering over the handwritten notes. It seemed to her that the cards grew more beautiful every year. She set them aside to show Tabitha later.

Next came the usual stack of flyers, charity requests, and advertisements. Then she reached the last envelope —one from the gas company. A red URGENT was stamped in the corner.

Her brow furrowed. She tore it open and scanned the notice. Her expression shifted from confusion to alarm. It was a disconnect notice—the gas bill hadn't been paid.

Laura shoved her chair back so fast it tipped over with a thud. Clutching the letter, she raced into the parlor.

"Gran—this says the gas bill hasn't been paid!" she exclaimed, holding up the paper.

Tabitha looked up, startled. "That can't be! The bank pays all our utilities automatically. You set that up yourself."

"That's right," Laura replied. "We're on autopay."

"Then there must be some mistake," Tabitha said

calmly, closing her book. "The gas company has it wrong." She paused, biting her lip. "Unless …"

Laura's pulse quickened. "Unless what?"

Tabitha's eyes shifted uneasily. "Unless maybe there *was* a problem."

"What kind of problem?"

"Well …" Tabitha frowned in concentration. "I got a call from the bank while you were in Chicago."

Laura's stomach dropped. "Who called you from the bank? And what did they want?"

"That nice Catherine," Tabitha said.

Laura's blood ran cold. "How did you know it was Catherine?"

"She gave me her name, of course—and I recognized her voice."

Laura took a steadying breath. "What did Catherine say?"

"She said someone was trying to get into my accounts and steal my money," Tabitha explained.

"And?" Laura's voice trembled.

"I told her you were out of town and I couldn't get to the bank, so she offered to go online and make sure everything was safe."

Laura felt her knees weaken and sank onto the sofa. "What else, Gran?"

"Catherine asked me for my login information—my username and password."

Laura's voice hardened. "Did you give them to her?"

"Oh, yes," Tabitha said brightly. "She was so nice about it. She even waited while I went to get the paper where we'd written it down. I offered to call her back, but she said there wasn't time—we needed to act fast."

Laura's ears began to ring.

"Is something wrong, dear?" Tabitha asked, her brow creasing. "Catherine said she stopped the thieves in time. Everything was fine."

"There should be tens of thousands of dollars in your checking account," Laura said numbly. "Plenty to pay the gas bill."

"As I said," Tabitha reiterated, "maybe it's just a billing mistake."

Laura forced herself to stand. "Why didn't you tell me about that call when I got home—or tell Kurt or Clara while I was gone?"

"I didn't think there was anything wrong," Tabitha said, sitting up straighter. "And when you got back, there was so much going on, I just forgot."

Laura pressed her lips together. "All right. I'll check your accounts online now. I should have done that when I got home."

"You've been busy with that new man of yours," Tabitha teased softly. "It's nice to see you having fun for once."

Laura didn't answer. Her hands shook as she opened

her laptop on the kitchen table. She typed the password wrong—twice—before the bank's website loaded. Her breath caught as she clicked on Accounts.

Three entries appeared: one for checking, one for savings, and one for an investment account. All showed a balance of $0.00.

Laura stared at the screen, unblinking. The room tilted slightly. She swallowed hard to keep from being sick. She'd read about scams like this. She and Tabitha had done everything right—or so she'd thought. But whoever had called hadn't been Catherine from the bank.

Tabitha Trent had been robbed of her life's savings.

"Everything all right, dear?" Tabitha called from the parlor. "Did you find the money?"

Laura closed her eyes and drew in a long breath. The bank was closed until Friday. Nothing could be done tonight. Tomorrow was Thanksgiving—and she refused to destroy what might be her grandmother's last one.

She slammed the laptop shut and stood. The oven buzzer rang, signaling the pie was done.

Laura stepped into the doorway and forced a smile. "Don't worry, Gran. Everything will be fine."

Tabitha's sharp eyes narrowed. "You're sure?"

"I'm sure," Laura said. "I'm going to take the pies out of the oven—and then I'm taking that nap."

Thanksgiving morning dawned gray and cold. Thin sunshine in the late afternoon disappeared behind a veil of ominous storm clouds by the time Laura, Tabitha, and Ian arrived at Johanson's Diner. Strings of autumn garland framed the big plate-glass windows, and the scent of roasted turkey greeted them as they stepped out of their car in the parking lot.

Inside, the place buzzed with laughter and conversation. Maisie and Josef were already seated in their usual corner booth, their faces flushed with warmth and good cheer. Across from them, Clara and Kurt waved, motioning for Laura, Tabitha, and Ian to join them.

"Happy Thanksgiving!" Clara said, sliding out of her seat to hug each of them. "Are you hungry?"

"Starved," Tabitha said with a twinkle. "It smells wonderful in here."

Laura forced a smile and murmured her agreement, though her appetite had deserted her hours ago. She'd spent most of the day pretending everything was fine, forcing herself to set the table for Brad's visit that evening, steam the wrinkles from her dress, and banter cheerfully with Tabitha about the Macy's parade. It had been an act of will to walk out the door without blurting out the truth.

Their server arrived with platters filled with their pre-ordered dinner. Everyone joined hands and lowered their heads while Josef said grace. Conversation flowed easily as they worked their way through roast turkey, stuffing, mashed potatoes, sweet potatoes, and the usual fixings. They discussed the success of the Thanksgiving food drive, the record-breaking days at Sweets & Treats, and Kurt's upcoming renovation project. Ian chimed in with his ideas for turning the guest house attic into a bedroom. Laura nodded in all the right places but barely registered the words. The letter from the gas company, folded in her purse, felt like a weight she couldn't set down.

"Are you okay?" Clara asked Laura, noticing her distraction. "You're quiet tonight."

Laura blinked. "Oh—just tired," she said, reaching for her water. "It's been a long week."

Kurt commiserated. "Join the club."

Tabitha sighed contentedly. "Now this," she said, "is my idea of a perfect Thanksgiving."

Maisie reached across the table to squeeze her hand. "We're thankful your family is here, Tabitha. You've become part of our family, too."

"Indeed, you have," Josef added warmly.

As dessert was served—pumpkin pie with whipped cream—Clara raised her glass. "To new beginnings," she said. "A new husband, home, and another year surrounded by the people I love best."

"Hear, hear," Kurt said, tapping his glass against hers.

Laura joined in, echoing their toast, though her voice caught. She looked across the table at her grandmother. Tabitha was laughing at something Josef had said, her eyes shining, her smile easy and unguarded.

Tomorrow, she'd call the bank the moment it opened and do whatever it took to fix what had happened. But tonight, for Tabitha's sake, Thanksgiving would remain unblemished.

"Would you like another piece of pie?" Josef smiled at Ian. "You polished that one off in three bites."

Ian shook his head. "I shouldn't go for seconds."

Josef chuckled. "At your age, I could eat a dinner like

this and still be hungry. Enjoy it while you can, son. By the time you're as old as I am, you don't dare eat second helpings." Josef patted his stomach and waved to their server.

He approached their table with a coffeepot to refill their cups, and Josef ordered a second piece of pie for Ian. "Make it an extra-large slice," he added.

Laura got up from the table, murmuring that she was going to the ladies' room.

Clara pushed back her chair, saying that she would join her.

When they stood next to each other washing their hands, Clara turned to face Laura. "All right," she said. "What's going on? You have circles under your eyes as dark as today's storm clouds, and you were distracted all afternoon. Don't tell me it's fatigue."

Laura blinked rapidly, the corners of her eyes moist.

"You can tell me anything, Laura. You know that."

Laura drew a shaky breath. "It's Gran," she said finally. "Someone called her pretending to be from the bank. She gave them her login information. All of it."

Clara's stomach dropped. "Oh, Laura."

"I checked her account last night," Laura said, her voice breaking. "Everything's gone. The savings. The checking. Her investments. *Everything.*"

Clara put a hand on Laura's elbow. "Does Tabitha know?"

Laura shook her head. "No. And I can't tell her

tonight, Clara. It's Thanksgiving. You've seen her. She's so happy." Laura swiped at a tear. "I don't know what to do. I feel so helpless."

Clara's heart ached. "You did the right thing by telling me. We'll figure this out tomorrow. You're not alone in this."

They stood quietly for a moment before returning to the table, both of them wearing practiced smiles. When Kurt caught Clara's eye, she gave him the smallest shake of her head. *Later.*

Josef and Maisie had admitted they were exhausted and, at Kurt and Clara's urging, departed. Laura, Tabitha, and Ian had also gone home, Tabitha none the wiser. The diner had emptied out, and the staff was stacking chairs when Clara and Kurt finally slipped out into the crisp night air.

Kurt opened the car door for Clara. "There's something we need to talk about," she said.

He frowned. "That sounds ominous."

"It is. Get in and I'll explain." Clara told him everything on their drive back to the guest house.

When she finished, Kurt exhaled slowly. "Holy cow." He rubbed the back of his neck. "So the scammer wiped her out completely?"

"Every penny," Clara said.

"We both get scam emails and phone calls in our businesses every day," Kurt replied. "There's so much of this going on. It sounds like they tricked Tabitha using an artificial intelligence-generated voice that sounded like Catherine."

"That's what I think happened." Clara agreed. "Laura's going to the bank first thing tomorrow."

"I'll go with her," Kurt said immediately. "She'll need someone there."

Clara nodded, her throat tight. "She'll appreciate that. She's holding it together for Tabitha's sake, but she's scared to death."

"I can imagine. I hate to say it, Clara, but she shouldn't get her hopes up. Once that money's gone …" He shook his head. "It's impossible to get it back. We'll file a police report, but I don't hold out much hope."

Clara stared out the window. "I know," she said. "But we've got to try everything."

Kurt reached over and took her hand. "We'll help them through it. One way or another."

She nodded, blinking back tears. The future that had seemed so bright this morning now felt shrouded in clouds as dark as those in the night sky.

CHAPTER 23

"Thanks for coming with me this morning. I know how busy you are." Laura turned away from the passenger window to face Kurt. "I was so relieved when I got Clara's text last night saying you'd accompany me to the bank."

Kurt flipped on his turn signal and pulled into the parking lot. "Of course. I wouldn't want you to go through this alone."

"I called the bank first thing," Laura said. "I spoke to Catherine—she's working today. Patricia, Gran's new account manager, is out, but Catherine said she'd meet us at nine-thirty."

"You told her what happened?"

"I did."

"Did she have anything to say?"

Laura shook her head. "She said she was taking notes and wanted me to come in as soon as possible."

"Good," Kurt said. "I'm sure she's already alerted their fraud team."

They parked and walked through the glass doors into the quiet lobby. Patricia and Catherine were waiting near the reception desk.

"I thought you were off today," Laura said as they approached.

"I was," Patricia said, her expression somber. "But when Catherine called, I knew I needed to be here."

"Patricia, this is my friend Kurt Holbrook," Laura said. "He's an attorney and our neighbor."

Kurt shook hands with both women. "Nice to meet you."

"Let's go into my office," Patricia said. "Can I get you coffee?"

They declined, and she led them around a glass partition. Patricia took her seat behind the desk while Catherine stood behind her. Laura and Kurt sat in chairs across from Patricia.

Laura looked from one woman to the other. "There's no mistake, is there?" she asked. "The money's gone."

Patricia hesitated, then nodded. "I'm afraid so."

Laura turned to Catherine. "You never called Tabitha about someone trying to get into her accounts?"

Catherine's face tightened. "I did not. But I know how this happened. My voice must have been cloned using AI. Fraudsters are doing it everywhere now. You hear about it on the news—fake ransom calls and such."

Laura dropped her gaze to her lap.

"I'm so very sorry," Catherine said.

"Everyone here at the bank is devastated for you," Patricia added.

Kurt leaned forward. "Have you been able to trace where the money went?"

"It was transferred into offshore accounts," Patricia said. "I've already alerted our national security team and started the reports. That's why I came in today. Even though it's been weeks since the fraud happened, I didn't want to lose another day."

Laura's voice trembled. "Do you think we'll get any of it back?"

Patricia shifted in her chair while Catherine looked away. "It's highly unlikely," Patricia admitted. "But we'll make every effort. The authorities have been notified. They'll need a statement from Tabitha."

A small sob escaped Laura. "She doesn't know yet," she said. "I found out when the gas company sent a past-due notice. She still thinks the billing is a mistake. I don't know how to tell her she's been scammed. She's always been so proud of managing her money carefully."

Catherine's eyes glistened. "I've known Tabitha for more than thirty years. She's meticulous—one of the most responsible clients I've ever worked with. I'm devastated this happened to her."

Kurt interjected. "Would you mind if I acted as the contact person for the bank and law enforcement? I'll coordinate the exchange of information. Tabitha will have to be told, of course, but that doesn't need to happen today."

Laura nodded gratefully. "Thank you. I need some time to figure out how to tell her."

"Would you like me to help when the time comes?" he asked Laura.

"That would help," she replied, then turned back to Patricia and Catherine. "Thank you both for meeting with us."

Kurt pulled a business card from his wallet and jotted a number on the back before handing it to Patricia. "This is my personal cell phone number. Please call me with any updates."

Patricia tucked the card into her drawer. "You'll know as soon as I learn anything."

As they stood to leave, Catherine followed them to the door. "I feel terrible that the scammers used my voice to defraud Tabitha," she said, her voice thick with emotion. "Please know how sorry I am."

Laura managed a wan smile. "This isn't your fault, Catherine. You were a victim, too."

Catherine nodded. "Even so, I'm heartsick for all of you."

Kurt circled the block twice before finally finding a parking spot along the curb. He picked up the container holding two turkey sandwiches—layered with stuffing and cranberry sauce —from the passenger seat. To round out the meal, he'd stopped at Pinewood General Store for bags of chips and a couple of sodas.

It was 10:30 when he stepped through the door of Sweets & Treats, hoping to steal a few minutes with his wife before the lunchtime rush. He'd slept in until nine that Saturday morning and skipped breakfast, so he was more than ready to eat. Since Clara had been at work since 4:30 a.m., he knew she'd welcome an early lunch as well.

Six customers stood in line at the counter while two of Clara's employees boxed pastries into the shop's signature pink boxes. Her workers smiled and nodded when they spotted him slipping behind the counter and into the workroom.

The industrial-sized mixer hummed along one wall while Joan and two other bakers piped jewel-colored macarons. Clara, her cheeks pink from the heat of the ovens, was moving golden baguettes to cooling racks. She turned and smiled when he called her name.

"Good morning," she said. "I thought you and Laura were going to talk to Tabitha this morning."

Kurt shook his head. "She texted to say she's not ready yet. She wants to go through her own finances with a fine-tooth comb before saying anything."

"That sounds ominous," Clara replied. "Did she elaborate?"

"No," Kurt said. "But the upkeep and taxes on that big old house of Tabitha's must be substantial—not to mention the utilities. I wonder if they can manage on a teacher's salary."

"Oh, my gosh," Clara said. "That's awful."

"I'm just speculating," Kurt said. "Let's not worry about it until we know for sure."

"Okay," Clara replied. "I've got enough on my mind right now—with the bakery and the new house." She rolled the cooling racks of baguettes aside and nodded toward the paper grocery bag and plastic container in his hands. "What have you got there?"

"Lunch," he said with a grin. "For both of us."

"Really? Once again, you're the perfect husband. I'm starving."

"I made us those leftover turkey sandwiches you love. I hope I got them right."

"Anything made with love is always good," Clara said, smiling.

"Looks like you've been busy."

Clara's face lit up. "Run off our feet all morning! I thought everyone would be at the mall Christmas shopping, but we've had lines since we opened."

"Same at all the downtown shops," Kurt said. "I had to circle the block twice to park."

"Let's pull up a couple of chairs at my desk," Clara said. "We can wolf this down, then I'll get back to work."

"Any chance you could step out for an hour?"

Clara widened her eyes. "No way. I'm lucky to get five minutes to eat. I haven't even had a bathroom break since I got here."

"I thought you'd say that," Kurt said with a smile. "Dan called this morning. He wants us to meet him at his office at noon."

"Did he say why?"

"No, but I'm guessing it's about the new house."

"Can you go without me? I can't get away until Monday, when Sweets & Treats is closed."

"Sure," Kurt said, handing her a sandwich and a bag of chips.

Clara took a big bite. "This is the quintessential Thanksgiving-leftover sandwich," she said around a mouthful.

Kurt grinned. "Glad it passed muster."

She gave him a thumbs-up as she kept eating.

"Clara!" Joan called from across the room. "The oven temperature won't hold steady again!"

Clara groaned good-naturedly and stood. "Thanks for bringing lunch—and making it so wonderful," she said. "I've got to tinker with that finicky oven, but you can bet I'll finish this sandwich as soon as I can."

"I'll text you after I meet with Dan," Kurt said, tossing his empty chip bag and soda can in the trash.

Clara leaned in to kiss him before turning back to the bustle of the workroom.

"This is terrible news," Kurt said.

Dan sat across the conference table from him and nodded with a frown. "I'm so sorry. I've been a realtor for almost forty years, and I've never seen this happen before."

"I've done my share of probate work," Kurt said. "I've even handled a few contested wills. But someone signing contracts as the executor of an estate who didn't actually have the authority to sign? That's a first."

"It doesn't change the outcome," Dan said. "He thought he was authorized. The restraining order and lawsuit from the other family members came after he told them he'd sold the house."

Kurt skimmed the court papers again, his jaw tightening.

"You're a lawyer," Dan said. "You'd know best how to dispute their claim that the contract isn't valid. You don't have to agree with their assertion."

Kurt tossed the papers onto the table. "I know," he replied, "but we could be tied up in litigation for years." He shook his head. "I don't want that. Clara and I need to buy a house and move forward. This, apparently, isn't the one."

"Honestly," Dan said, "I think that's wise."

"Thank you, Dan," Kurt said. "I appreciate you coming in on a Saturday—on Thanksgiving weekend, no less—to give me the bad news in person."

"Of course," Dan replied. "How do you think Clara will take it?"

"That's the worst part," Kurt admitted. "She had her heart set on that house. She'll be devastated. But she'll understand—we need to let it go."

"There's nothing else on the market right now," Dan said, "but that can change in an instant. I'll keep talking to my network of other realtors, and you'll be the first to know when something new is about to be listed. If there's one thing I've learned in this business, it's that things can turn around fast."

Kurt nodded through the disappointment in his eyes. "Let's hope so," he murmured.

CHAPTER 25

Brad pulled into Laura's driveway and stopped beside the walkway to the front door. "Where have you been all evening?" he asked, turning to face her.

"What do you mean? I've been right here with you."

"Your body has been," he said, tapping his temple, "but not your mind. You've been somewhere else the entire time."

She turned toward the passenger-side window, avoiding his gaze.

"You were distracted on Thanksgiving night when I came over for pie," he continued. "I believed you when you said you were tired. And again tonight? You've been distant the whole evening."

"No … I …"

Brad reached across the center console and laid his

hand gently on her elbow. "I thought we had something special, Laura. Honestly, I'm falling for you, big time. If I've misread things, I want you to tell me now. I'll say good night and won't bother you again."

She swung around to face him, eyes wide. "I do like you," she said. "*Really* like you. You're the best thing that's happened to me in years. It's just that I've had some extremely distressing—catastrophic, even—news. I've been trying to figure out what to do about it."

"That's awful," Brad said, leaning toward her. "I had no idea. Does it involve Tabitha?"

Laura nodded.

"Is she ill?"

"No. Physically she's fine, and you've met her—she's as sharp as a tack. But she's gotten herself into a horrible financial situation. Both of us, actually."

He compressed his lips into a tight line.

"I spent Friday and today going through our financial papers and have come up with a solution. It's not ideal, but it's the only thing I can think of."

"What does Tabitha say about it?"

Laura bit her lower lip. "That's just it. I haven't told her yet."

"I see," he said. "Would you like to tell me about it? My grandmother always said, 'A burden shared is a burden halved.'"

A small smile tugged at Laura's lips. "Gran says that,

too. If you don't mind, I would like to tell you. I'm not looking for answers or alternatives—I've made up my mind—but talking to you might help me figure out how to tell her."

"I'm a good listener," Brad said. "And I'll keep anything you share in the strictest confidence."

Laura studied his kind, earnest face. "This'll take a while," she said. "Let's go inside. We've got half a pumpkin pie in the fridge. Would you like a slice?"

"I'd never turn that down," he said, smiling.

"Good. You can eat while I talk."

They climbed out of the car and closed the doors, the sound echoing in the still night. Laura led him around the side of the house and up the steps to the back door. She slipped her key into the lock and it opened with a loud click. They stepped through the back hallway and into the dark kitchen.

"I could've sworn the kitchen light was on when we came up the steps," she murmured.

Brad shrugged. "I didn't notice."

Laura pulled the pie from the refrigerator and served a generous slice to him. "Whipped cream?" she asked.

"What kind of question is that?" he said with a grin. "Of course I want whipped cream."

She handed him the canister of Reddi Whip. "Sorry, we don't have homemade. I'll let you do the honors."

He squirted a mound of whipped cream onto his pie

and returned the canister to the refrigerator. "Tell me everything," he said.

She sat across from him, took a steadying breath, and launched into the heartbreaking story.

TABITHA SETTLED into her chair in the parlor after Brad had picked up Laura for their date. She knew her granddaughter was head over heels for him, and she guessed he felt the same way about Laura. Still, her granddaughter had been subdued the entire day.

When Tabitha had asked Laura about the mound of paperwork scattered across the kitchen table, she had replied she was "getting a jump on organizing her tax papers." Laura had been a truthful child, and Tabitha had always known when she was lying. She was certain her granddaughter wasn't telling her the truth now.

Sighing, Tabitha picked up her book and began to read.

Ian came downstairs at nine o'clock. "What are you doing up, Gran?" he asked.

"Reading," she said, gesturing with her book. "I'm not tired, and this one's a real page-turner. I can't put it down."

He grinned. "I'm getting a piece of pie. Then I'm heading to bed."

"That's a wonderful idea," she said. "Pie and an early bedtime are always a winning plan."

"Would you like a slice?"

"No, but thank you."

He disappeared into the kitchen. Tabitha waited until she heard the click of his bedroom door closing after he headed upstairs. This was the moment she'd been waiting for. She put her book aside and went into the kitchen.

The papers Laura was working through were neatly stacked on the small desk in the corner. Tabitha carried them to the kitchen table, perched her reading glasses on her nose, and began her investigation. It was nearly eleven o'clock when she heard car doors slam in the driveway. "Good heavens," she murmured, glancing at the clock.

She snatched the papers, not caring if they were in order, straightened the stack as best she could, and returned them to the desk. As she turned out the kitchen light, she heard footsteps on the back stairs. Tabitha slipped out of the kitchen, past the downstairs bathroom, and into her darkened bedroom. She was easing the door closed when she heard Brad's voice from the kitchen.

"Tell me everything."

Tabitha froze, her hand on the doorknob. She leaned forward, pressing her ear toward the hallway. At first, she could barely make out Laura's words. But as her granddaughter's emotions rose, her voice grew louder.

"Bottom line, we can't keep living the way we have. My salary as a high school teacher and the rent from the guest house only cover about a third of what we need to maintain this house." Her voice caught. "I promised my mother, on her deathbed, that I'd take care of Gran and make sure she could live out her days here."

"That's a kind thing," Brad said, "but situations change."

"I know," Laura replied, her tone anguished. "But Gran lived her entire adult life in this house. She and my grandfather raised their children here. I'm afraid it would kill her to move. I can't let that happen."

"So what do you propose?"

"I think Gran, Ian, and I should move into the guest house and rent out this one. It won't bring in enough to cover all our expenses, but I've got other funds. I inherited a modest amount from my mother, which I put in a college fund for Ian. I could use some of that to help us stay here."

"I haven't been inside the guest house," Brad said, "but it looks small."

"It's two bedrooms and one bath," Laura explained. "Kurt and Ian discovered that the attic could be finished into another bedroom. Ian's excited about it—he was telling Josef all about it at Thanksgiving dinner. It'll be tight for the three of us, but, if we can turn that attic into a bedroom, we'll manage."

"I'd be happy to help with that," Brad said.

"Thank you," Laura said. "Ian's eager to pitch in, too. I'll pay you for your time and materials, of course."

"Don't worry about that," he said. "What about Kurt and Clara?"

"I know it'll be inconvenient for them," Laura said. "But I'll ask them to vacate the guest house in January, after Clara's busy season at Sweets & Treats. At least they have Kurt's place to move into."

Brad hesitated. "Didn't they tell you? Kurt sold his house. A new family's already moved in."

"No." Laura brought her hand to her forehead. "I guess we've all been so busy." Laura was silent for a moment. "Well," she said finally, "I'm not going to force them out before they can move into their new home. I'll dig deeper into my savings until then."

"I know Kurt and Clara," Brad said. "They wouldn't want you to do that. They'll find somewhere to rent during renovations. Some people put a pre-owned manufactured home on the lot and live there while construction is ongoing. It makes it easier to monitor progress."

"Really?"

"Yep. Happens all the time," he said with a reassuring smile.

"Okay," Laura said slowly. "I'll think about it—and about talking to Gran."

The grandfather clock in the hallway chimed midnight.

"It sounds like you've made your decisions," Brad said.

"I have," Laura replied. "Thank you for listening. It's helped me sort through things."

They pushed back their chairs and stood.

"Please don't say anything to Kurt and Clara about this," she added.

"I won't," Brad promised. "You can count on me."

Laura walked him to the back door, and Tabitha closed her bedroom door, her heart pounding. Her worst fears had been confirmed—and she knew exactly what she had to do.

CHAPTER 26

Tabitha replaced the receiver on the phone in the parlor, then closed her eyes and leaned back in her chair. A faint smile played on her lips. Talking over her latest problem with her lifelong best friend had given her the clarity she needed. Maisie had also shared some important information. Between the two of them, they realized they were the only people who possessed all the pieces of the puzzle. Together, they created a plan that both of them agreed was divinely inspired.

The sound of footsteps on the stairs interrupted Tabitha's reverie. She opened her eyes just as Laura entered the room.

"Gran, you're dressed for church already?"

"Yes," Tabitha replied. "I'm going to the early service this morning. Josef and Maisie are picking me up. I was just about to go into the kitchen to leave you a note." She gestured toward the window seat. "After church, I'm going back to Maisie's to help her fix a dropped stitch in a complicated Fair Isle pattern. I'm bringing my knitting, too."

Her knitting bag and purse lay on the window seat. "Maisie and I will knit the afternoon away in front of the fire," Tabitha continued. "She's invited all of us—including Brad, by the way, if you wish to mention it to him—to join them for dinner. Clara and Kurt will be there, too."

"That's awfully nice of her," Laura said, covering her mouth to stifle a yawn.

"You've been working so hard on the …" Tabitha hesitated for a moment, then finished delicately, "on the taxes. I knew you'd be happy not to cook tonight. What are you doing today?"

"Brad is taking Ian and me to buy our Christmas tree," Laura said. "Ian's always wanted a live tree, and I decided this would be the year." She glanced toward the bay window, remembering the huge trees from her childhood that had nearly brushed the twelve-foot ceiling.

"That's a wise decision," Tabitha said warmly.

Laura gave her a curious look.

Tabitha bit her lip and smiled faintly.

"I'll invite Brad to join us and let you know."

"We'll set a place for him unless we hear otherwise."

"There's something I need to talk to you about," Laura said, squaring her shoulders. "It's serious."

"Good heavens," Tabitha replied. "I'm afraid it'll have to wait until tonight. Maisie and Josef will be here any minute. In fact …" She cocked her head. "It sounds like they're pulling into the driveway now."

Laura crossed to the window and pulled back the curtain. "They're here," she confirmed.

"Then we'll talk as soon as we get home tonight," Tabitha assured her. "Would you mind handing me my purse and knitting bag?"

"I'll carry them to the car for you," Laura said.

The two women walked outside together. Tabitha settled herself into the back seat while Laura handed her the purse and knitting bag.

Tabitha touched her granddaughter's arm. "You look like you're carrying the weight of the world on your shoulders, dear. Enjoy your afternoon with your son and that boyfriend you're so smitten with. Things may not be as bad as they seem."

"THIS IS ABSOLUTELY DELICIOUS, MRS. JOHANSON," Brad said, covering his mouth with his hand.

"Please," she replied with a laugh. "It's Maisie—and

I'm glad you enjoyed it. I thought we could use a change after all the poultry of the last few days. It's a new recipe, which is risky when you're inviting people over for dinner."

"It's like the perfect marriage between beef stew and French onion soup," Clara said. "The croutons and the gooey Gruyère are fabulous. There's Parmesan in here, too, isn't there?"

Maisie nodded.

"The salad and breadsticks were the only accompaniments you needed," Tabitha said. "You've done it again, Maisie—another spectacular meal."

"Tabitha and I made a batch of Christmas shortbread cookies for dessert," Maisie added.

"I'll start the coffee," Josef said, rising from the table.

Kurt sprang to his feet, followed by Ian and Brad.

"Our job is to clear the table and do the dishes," Ian said knowledgeably to Brad.

"Just clear the plates and bring the coffee and cookies to the table," Maisie said. She glanced at Tabitha, who nodded her head. "Tabitha has something she'd like to say to everyone."

All eyes turned to the old woman. Tabitha smiled sweetly at the group.

Laura and Clara exchanged glances across the table. Laura shrugged, and Clara widened her eyes. They joined the men in clearing the dishes, then returned to their seats.

A steaming mug of coffee sat in front of each person, and the plate of buttery cookies had made its way around the table when Tabitha rose to her feet.

Everyone gave her their attention. She looked from face to face, drinking in the love and concern reflected there. "I believe all of you—except perhaps Ian—know that I fell victim to a scammer several weeks ago. They defrauded me of every penny of my life savings. As devastating as that is, there's nothing to be done. I understand I won't get any of my money back."

No one moved.

"I can no longer afford to live in my grand old home —the house I've loved my entire life."

"No … Gran …" Laura leaned forward in her chair.

Tabitha raised a hand to stop her. "Things happen in life that we don't expect and certainly don't welcome. But we must deal with them, nonetheless. I've learned that what first appears to be a disaster often turns into a blessing. This may be one of those times. I've decided to sell my home."

Clara gasped. "Oh, Tabitha, I'm so sorry to hear that. You must be devastated. I wish we weren't already under contract on that look-alike house on the other side of the square. I'd much rather have the real thing."

Tabitha and Maisie exchanged a conspiratorial smile, then looked at Kurt.

"About that," Kurt said, grinning from ear to ear.

Clara's eyebrows shot up. "What?"

"Our deal fell through," he said. "That's what Dan wanted to talk about yesterday. The heirs are currently in litigation, which is tying up the estate that's selling the property."

Clara clasped her hands together and brought them to her chest. "So … this means we can buy Tabitha's house?"

He nodded.

"That's the best news!" she exclaimed. Then, narrowing her eyes, she added, "When were you going to tell me?"

"You've been so busy at the patisserie that I decided to wait until tonight," he said. "Tomorrow's your day off —I figured you'd be heartbroken and would need the day to recover."

"You're right about that," Clara said. "If it weren't for this better news, I'd have spent the whole day in bed, feeling sorry for myself."

"There's more," Maisie said, joining the conversation. "Tabitha, Laura, and Ian will need a place to live. They were wondering if you'd like to keep the guesthouse as an income-producing property."

"And rent to them?" Kurt asked.

Clara turned to him, her face glowing. "That's a marvelous idea! Don't you think so?"

He nodded, smiling wider. "We'll simply be swapping houses. No moving company needed!" He looked at Ian. "We'll carry everything between the two houses ourselves."

"Count me in, too," Brad said.

Kurt grinned. "And now, Ian," he said, "we can get busy and turn that attic into your bedroom."

"Really?" the boy cried.

"It'd be a pretty tight squeeze for the three of you if we don't," Kurt said. "Besides, it'll be a more valuable rental if it's three bedrooms and two baths." He turned to Brad. "How long do you think it would take to add a bathroom upstairs and finish the attic?"

"I'll need to take a look at the space, of course," Brad replied. "But since I'm not doing a full renovation on that historical house across the square"—he shot Kurt a teasing look—"my crew can start this project right away."

"Good," Kurt said. "I think the most practical thing is for Clara and me to stay in the guesthouse until those changes are finished. After that, we'll make our moves."

Clara hugged Kurt, then went to throw her arms around Laura. "I'm so happy we'll still be close neighbors!"

"It sounds like we're all in agreement," Tabitha said,

looking around the table. Everyone nodded. She smiled and sank into her chair. "I'm glad we've got this decided. But now, I'm suddenly very tired. I hate to eat and run, but I need to say good night."

"There's just one more thing," Josef said. "I've got an early Christmas present for someone—and I think he's going to need it in the next few weeks." He rose from the table and returned with a large rectangular box wrapped in Christmas paper and topped with a shiny bow.

"I wrapped it myself," Josef said, handing the box to Ian.

The package was heavy, and Ian almost dropped it. He looked up, eyes wide.

"During Thanksgiving dinner, you told us about your ideas for that attic," Josef said. "And you were eager to do some of the work yourself. Well, it looks like you're going to get the chance."

Ian tore off the paper and opened the box. Inside was a brand-new carpenter's tool belt, complete with a hammer, tape measure, utility knife, pencils, speed square, and nail set.

"That should get you started," Josef said.

Ian jumped to his feet and buckled the belt around his waist.

Brad leaned in to inspect it. "That's a legit tool belt," he said. "It's as nice as the one I've got. You can keep that for your lifetime."

Kurt stood, and soon the four men were deep in conversation about the upcoming renovation.

Tabitha and Maisie shared a knowing smile.

Laura stepped away from Clara. "I'd better take Gran home," she said. "To be honest, I'm dead on my feet, too. I didn't sleep a wink last night, worrying about how to tell her we couldn't afford to stay in the house."

"Kurt and I will bring Ian home," Clara said. "We'll clean up the kitchen before we head out."

Laura retrieved her grandmother's knitting bag, purse, and coat. "You were right again, Gran."

Tabitha raised her eyebrows. "About what, dear?"

"You always said people waste a lot of time worrying about things that never happen," Laura said. "That's exactly what I've been doing."

Tabitha patted Laura's arm. "That's a lesson we spend our whole lives learning," she said. "As it turns out, we've got nothing but good days ahead of us."

The End

THANK YOU FOR READING

If you enjoyed *Pies & Plans,* I'd be grateful if you wrote a review.

Just a few lines on Amazon or Goodreads would be great. Reviews are the best gift an author can receive. They encourage us when they're good, help us improve our next book when they're not, and help other readers make informed choices when purchasing books. Goodreads reviews help readers find new books. Reviews on Amazon keep the Amazon algorithms humming and are the most helpful aide in selling books! Thank you.

To post a review on Amazon:

1. Go to the product detail page for *Pies & Plans* on Amazon.com.

2. Click "Write a customer review" in the Customer Reviews section.

3. Write your review and click Submit.

172

In gratitude,
Barbara Hinske

CHARACTER LIST

Main Characters

Clara Conway

Owner and head baker of *Sweets & Treats*. In her early thirties, Clara is talented, hardworking, and quietly romantic.

Kurt Holbrook

Local attorney and downtown property owner. Tall and steady with an easy smile, Kurt is thoughtful, pragmatic, and deeply supportive.

Noelle

Clara's terrier–dachshund mix with an outsized personality. Mostly white with brown markings and endlessly expressive eyes, Noelle is fiercely loyal, slightly dramatic, and Clara's constant companion.

The Pinewood Circle

Maisie Johanson

Former diner baker and Clara's mentor. Maisie becomes Clara's silent partner in *Sweets & Treats* and a beloved maternal presence.

Josef Johanson

Maisie's husband and owner of Johanson's Diner. Practical, kind, and business-savvy, Josef offers Clara guidance, encouragement, and steady support.

Joan

Senior baker at *Sweets & Treats*.

Laura Ramsey

High-school chemistry teacher and Clara's close friend.

Ian Ramsey

Laura's son.

Tabitha Trent

Laura's grandmother and Ian's great-grandmother. Tabitha lives in a stately Victorian home near the downtown square.

Friends, Neighbors, and Colleagues

Brad

Contractor, Kurt's best friend, and property manager.

Betty

Long-time diner baker who transitions to *Sweets & Treats*.

Susan

Baker at *Sweets & Treats* who also manages the shop's social media presence.

Amy

Owner of *The Keepsake Closet*, a vintage clothing shop on the town square.

Pam and Paula

Sisters who own *Briarwood Kitchen*, a farm-to-table restaurant outside Pinewood.

Robert, Patricia, and Catherine

Employees of Pinewood Bank. Robert is Tabitha's longtime banker; Patricia replaces him upon his retirement; Catherine remains as a trusted assistant.

Dan

The real-estate agent who assists Clara and Kurt.

Andy Rodriguez

Owner of Andy's Automotive, the mechanic who helps Clara when she first arrives in Pinewood.

Josie

Works at the local no-kill animal shelter.

Mary

Server at Johanson's Diner, known for her bold magenta-and-black hair.

Nick

Owner of the guitar shop next door to *Sweets & Treats*.

Jack

Nick's elderly Golden Retriever with a gentle, friendly nature.

Jerry Brunk

Pinewood attorney who assists Clara with forming her business.

Mr. Barnes

Elderly widower who lives on the same street as Tabitha.

Sarah and Don

Maisie's sister and brother-in-law.

From Clara's Past

Travis Conway

Clara's ex-husband. A charming but manipulative dentist whose betrayal propels Clara to leave her old life behind.

Melanie

Travis's dental hygienist and affair partner.

Marilyn

Clara's former best friend from her hospital dietician days.

Tom

Marilyn's husband and the attorney who handled Clara's divorce.

ACKNOWLEDGMENTS

I'm blessed with the wisdom and support of many kind and generous people. I want to thank the most supportive and delightful group of champions an author could hope for:

My remarkable husband, Brian Willis, who never fails to steer me in the right direction when I'm stuck on a plot point;

My life coach Mat Boggs for your wisdom and guidance;

My kind and generous legal team, Kenneth Kleinberg, Esq., and Michael McCarthy—thank you for believing in my vision;

The professional "dream team" of my editors Linden Gross, Dione Benson, and proofreader Dana Lee;

Elizabeth Mackey for a beautiful cover.

PLEASE ENJOY THIS EXCERPT
FROM COMING TO ROSEMONT

PROLOGUE

Frank Haynes spotted the forlorn-looking creature in the trees at the side of the road. He quickly pulled his Mercedes sedan off the highway and buttoned his cashmere sport coat against the icy fog as he stepped out onto the grassy berm. He walked gingerly in his slick-bottomed dress shoes as he approached the thin calico lurking in the underbrush. The wary animal rose up on her front legs, ready to take flight, and eyed him uneasily.

Haynes crooned softly to her. He pulled his collar up against the biting wind and wished he had grabbed his topcoat out of the backseat. But he dare not move now. The cat gradually relaxed and cautiously picked her way to him over the frost-stiffened grass. The cat rubbed against his legs in the familiar figure-eight pattern and began to purr—a tiny, tentative whisper that ripened into a deep, throaty rumble.

He reached a cautious hand down to her. She stretched into him, and he knew the bond had been made. He scooped her up and cradled the filthy creature against his chest, shielding her from the cold and stroking her gently, unconcerned about his expensive coat. When she was content, he returned to his car and placed her carefully in the blanket-lined crate that lived in his backseat for just such occasions. "You're safe now," he whispered the assurance. "You won't have to worry about food or cold anymore."

He shut the mesh grate of the cage and was surprised when the cat curled up and went to sleep. Most strays meowed and screamed all the way to the no-kill shelter that Haynes had founded and currently funded.

As he slipped behind the steering wheel, Haynes automatically checked the cell phone left behind in the console and was shocked to see he missed six calls during the short time he had been rescuing the cat. All from Westbury's idiot mayor, William Wheeler. He punched the return call button as he swung back onto the highway. Wheeler picked up on the first ring.

"Frank—where have you been? All hell's going to break loose around here," Wheeler shouted into the phone.

"What's up?" Haynes replied calmly.

"The town treasurer just called and told me the town can't cover the December payments from the pension fund. We're in trouble, Frank."

Damn, Haynes thought. This was coming two months earlier than he predicted. They wouldn't have time to get any of the condos sold by December. "Have you talked to either of the Delgados?"

"I called Chuck to tell him to move money from the reserve account you guys told me about. He said to talk to Ron about it. Ron thinks the reserve account has been 'depleted.' Some accountant and financial advisor he is! How did you guys let this happen? What have you been up to? If the town doesn't make those payments, we're sunk."

"Don't worry about it. I'll call Chuck and we'll get it straightened out. We always do, don't we?" Haynes disconnected the call over Wheeler's sputtering response.

Damn this faltering real estate market and those greedy, careless Delgado brothers. How had they drained the reserve fund so quickly? They must be siphoning money for their own use from the tidy sum that the three of them had "borrowed" from the town worker's pension fund. Fleecing the faceless public was one thing. Double-crossing Frank Haynes was quite another. Wheeler was set up to take the fall, if it came to that. He could make the trail lead to the Delgados, too. Haynes vowed to find out where every nickel had gone. He executed a sharp U-turn and headed back to Town Hall.

CHAPTER 1

Maggie Martin settled herself in the back of the cab as the driver pulled away from the airport and into the thin sunshine of a late February afternoon. She nodded when he leaned back to tell her that Westbury was an hour's drive, and turned her attention to the countryside streaming by her window. She was in no mood for idle chatter with a taxi driver. The dormant farmland lay still and expectant. Occasional clumps of leafless trees were silhouetted against the storm clouds that soon filled the sky. Maggie was glad she had carefully folded and packed those extra sweaters.

She shivered in spite of the heat blasting from the vents and wondered how anyone could live in a cold climate. *Southern California might not have four seasons, but who in their right mind wanted winter?* Maggie chastised herself once again for even making this trip. She was behind in her work—she needed the billings—and she probably wouldn't find any answers, anyway.

As the monotonous scenery sped by, Maggie relived her final moments with Paul in the cardiac ICU. Wired and tubed, he was hooked up to the best equipment modern medicine had to offer. Their children, Mike and Susan, were both frantically making their way through traffic, but neither arrived in time. It had been Maggie and Paul at the very end. In his final moments, Paul rallied. He feebly squeezed Maggie's hand and repeated breathlessly, "Sorry. So sorry. House is for you." At least, that's what she thought he said. She had been crying, and the beeping monitors and wheezing oxygen machine made it impossible to hear.

She had been over this a million times. It hadn't made any sense because she knew their house was hers. Hadn't they just paid it off and thrown a burn-the-mortgage party with the kids? She had tried to reassure Paul, to quiet him, but he had been desperate to make his point. Maggie now understood Paul's deathbed confession. That's why she had decided to come to Rosemont before she listed it for sale. She needed to get answers; to make some sense of her life.

Maggie planned to go straight to her hotel in Westbury to try to get a good night's sleep before she and the realtor toured the house and signed the listing papers the next day. But her plane had arrived forty-five minutes early, the only advantage of the bumpy flight through strong tailwinds. God knows she was exhausted, having spent another sleepless night rehashing her sham of a marriage. But she was far too curious to get a glimpse of Rosemont to wait any longer.

As they passed the highway sign announcing the Westbury exit fourteen miles ahead, Maggie retrieved her house key from the zippered compartment of her purse, leaned forward, and instructed the driver to take her directly to Rosemont.

The cabbie, as it turned out, didn't need directions. "Everybody in these parts knows the place," he assured her. "It's been vacant for years," he continued as he caught her eye in his rearview mirror. "Do you know the owner?"

"I am the owner," Maggie replied with an assurance in her voice that surprised her. "Actually, I just inherited Rosemont. I'm going to put it on the market, but I'm awfully curious to see it. Since it'll still be light when we get there, I thought I'd like to see it on my own, before the realtor and I get together tomorrow."

The cabbie nodded slowly, digesting this news, as he flipped on his left-turn signal and turned into a long, tree-lined drive that wound its way up a steep hill. They rounded the final corner and Maggie gasped. At the end of a deep lawn was an elegant manor house of aristocratic proportions. Built of warm limestone, with regal multi-paned windows, a sharply pitched tile roof, and six chimneys, Rosemont had the kind of gracious good looks that never go out of style. Dazed, she handed him his fare, with a more-than-generous tip, and secured his promise to drop her luggage at her hotel and return for her in an hour.

Maggie dashed through the now falling sleet to the massive front door. The key fit smoothly into the lock but wouldn't turn. She tugged and jiggled the handle, to no effect. It wasn't moving. Maggie looked wistfully over her shoulder as the taxi took the last turn at the end of the drive and vanished beyond the trees. Why did she have to insist on coming here tonight? Impatience did her in every time.

She buttoned the top button of her coat, fished the cabbie's card out of her pocket, and unzipped her purse to retrieve her phone. She'd have to call him to come back now. It was too cold and damp outside to even walk around and look in the windows. Maggie tugged off one of her gloves with her teeth and punched in his number on her phone. She brought it to her ear and idly tried the lock one more time. She felt something shift under her hand and the sturdy lock yielded. The door creaked open. Maggie abruptly ended the call and stepped over the threshold.

Even in the gloomy light of a stormy dusk, the beauty of the house overwhelmed Maggie, and she knew, for perhaps the first time in her life, that she was home. And that nothing would ever be the same again.

The mahogany front door opened to a foyer that gave way to a generous living room. A stone fireplace with an ornately carved mantel dominated one side of the room, and a graceful stairway swept up the opposite wall to the second floor. An archway led to a room lined with bookcases. *An honest-to-goodness library, for Pete's sake,* Maggie thought.

She inched forward slowly, like a dog expecting to come to the end of its leash, and peered into the library. Although all of the furniture was draped in heavy muslin covers, the room was stunning with its six-foot-high fireplace, French doors to a patio, and a stained-glass window. "I've been transported to a movie set of an English manor house," Maggie whispered. She set her purse on a round table in the middle of the foyer and unbuttoned her coat.

The fatigue and apathy that had been Maggie's constant companions since Paul's death began to dissipate as she examined this elegant old house she had inherited. Paul had never mentioned owning an estate on fifteen acres in Westbury. At least not until his final moments. Maggie had learned there were a lot of things that Paul had never mentioned. Unlike the others, this one was a pleasant surprise.

The remainder of the first floor was comprised of a large dining room, butler's pantry, kitchen, breakfast room, laundry, maid's quarters, and a large, sunny room whose function she couldn't identify. It had a herringbone tile floor and was lined with floor-to-ceiling windows along one wall. A conservatory, maybe? *Holy cow*—did she actually own a home with a library and a conservatory? The perfect lines of the house were evident at every turn.

With mounting excitement, Maggie found the switch for the chandelier that lit the staircase and raced to the second floor. A spacious landing gave way to six separate bedroom suites. She opened the first door carefully and proceeded with increasing confidence. Each suite was lovely and distinct in its own way, with huge windows and a sitting room and bathroom for each bedroom. One had a balcony, two had fireplaces. "I actually own this place," she murmured to herself in shock. She was considering which bedroom she liked best when she thought she heard a door close below. Was it already time for the taxi to return for her? Could she possibly have been here for an hour?

Maggie tore down the stairs as surely as if she had been running down them all of her life and came face to face with a solidly built man wearing tidy work clothes. With a pounding heart but steady voice, Maggie demanded to know who he was and how he got into her house.

He stepped back and held up his hands. "I'm sorry to startle you, ma'am. I'm Sam Torres. Your realtor expected you tomorrow, and he asked me to come by today to air the house out a bit and make sure that everything was in working order. I've been in the basement for the past three hours fiddling with the furnace. I've got it going now. I'm surprised we didn't hear each other. I didn't mean to frighten you."

He paused a moment to wipe his hands on a rag. He was never very good at guessing ages; he figured she must be in her fifties, but couldn't tell which end of that age range she leaned to. She was wrapped in a down-filled coat and wore those enormous Australian boots that were so popular. His wife lived in hers from October to May. She had a pair of glasses perched on her nose and was now regarding him imperiously through them.

"Welcome to Rosemont," he continued. "I understand you plan to put it on the market right away?"

Something about his polite, calm manner soon put her at ease. Judging by his weathered skin and full head of gray hair, she guessed he must be a few years her senior. She extended her hand to introduce herself and told him that she was most definitely not going to sell this place. Sam looked at her sharply and started to reply but stopped himself. Then, to her own astonishment, she announced, "As soon as my taxi returns, I'm going to check out of my hotel and move in here. Tonight. Permanently." She reached for the banister, as if to steady herself, and turned aside. *What are you doing?* she thought to herself. *You can't just up and move here. Are you nuts? What do you need with a six-bedroom house? Your family is in California, and so is your work.*

Maggie glanced back; Sam Torres was regarding her carefully. She wondered if he could sense that her decision to move into the house that night had been made impetuously on the spot.

"In that case," he said, "I'd better give you a complete tour. You'll need to know where all the entrances, switches, and thermostats are located." He gestured toward the library and began by showing her how to unlock and open the cantankerous old French doors. Sam nodded in the direction of the fireplace. "You won't want to start a fire until all of these chimneys have been cleaned and checked. This house hasn't been lived in for more than a decade." Sam paused and turned to Maggie. "Are you sure you want to move in here tonight? Once the plumbing is in use again, you'll find almost everything leaks. And the place hasn't been cleaned in years. Wouldn't you like to get it fixed up first?"

"No, I can live with all of that for a few days. As long as the furnace works and the electricity and water are turned on, I can cope."

"This sleet is supposed to turn to snow. You might get stranded up here," he cautioned as he produced a business card that read, "Sam the Handyman." "Here's my card. My cell phone number is on there. Why don't you call me when you get back tonight, and I can stop by to make sure that the furnace is still running and you're all set?" he offered.

"Thank you—very kind of you—but no need to drag out here later. I'll be fine," Maggie assured him with a confidence she didn't feel. For some reason, she felt completely comfortable with this concerned stranger. "Truthfully, this is a rash decision on my part."

Sam nodded.

"I can't explain it. I've never done anything like this in my entire life. But every fiber of my being tells me this is the right thing to do. For once in my adult life, I'm going to follow my intuition."

Sam regarded Maggie intently, and a slow smile lightened his worried expression. "In that case, moving in is exactly what you should do. Sounds like divine intuition. You should follow it. And you can always call me if anything comes up. My wife and I live about ten minutes away."

"Thank you, Sam. That makes me feel more comfortable." As they resumed their tour, Maggie was secretly relieved that Sam was making sure all the windows and doors were locked and all the thermostats were set. His instructions were thorough and helpful. It was evident that he knew the house well. The first floor had warmed to room temperature by the time they returned to the front door.

"I appreciate all you've done," Maggie said. "I'm not a

dab hand at home repairs, so I'm sure I'll need your help on a regular basis. What do I owe you for today?" she asked as she turned toward her purse.

"Don't worry about that now," Sam said as he reached for the door. "We can settle up later. Would you like me to have the driveway plowed tomorrow?" She gratefully accepted. They said goodnight, and he headed out the door.

***

Later, in the eerie brightness of the nighttime snow-storm, Maggie and the taxi driver wrestled her suitcases and three bags of groceries to her front door. The driver helped her get them all inside and cautiously inquired if she would be okay there. She assured him she would be just fine, but she knew he doubted it, and, frankly, so did she. He had glanced at her in his rearview mirror occasionally on the drive out there and must have seen the waves of emotion surging through her. She went from feeling confident, intuitive, courageous, and sponta-neous one moment to terrified, impulsive, incompetent, and irrational the next. She was known for her level-headed, depend-able (and ultimately predictable) nature. Paul said he never wondered what she was thinking, and her kids swore they knew what she would say before she said it—and they were usually right. At times

Maggie felt proud of this—she was understood, knowable, transparent. At other times, she felt dull and unimaginative. Well—this decision would surely make jaws drop.

As the taxi crept up the driveway toward her new life, fear and doubt were gaining the upper hand. She cleared her throat and was about to instruct the driver to take her back to the hotel when they again rounded the corner, and there it was. The house. *Her* house. Imposing, dependable, welcoming, strong. She would craft a happy future here.

She paid the driver, walked up the stone steps, and shut and locked the front door behind her. She toyed with the idea of phoning one of her children to let them know she changed her plans but decided against it. They could call her cell if they needed her. She wanted to savor her brave decision and her first night in her new home without the intrusion of their opinions.

Maggie picked up her groceries and headed in the direction of the kitchen. Dusty and in need of a thorough cleaning to be sure, but what a glorious kitchen! Beautiful walnut cabinets adorned with furniture-maker details soared to the twelve-foot ceiling. A huge window over the antique French sink and a smaller window over an old-fashioned copper vegetable sink would make the room irresistibly cheerful in daytime. The appliances and fixtures were outdated and would need to be replaced, but it was still the most beautiful kitchen she had ever seen—much less owned. *People will really have high expectations of a meal fixed here,* she mused. *I used to be such a good cook. I wonder if I can still muster up anything that does justice to this kitchen? I'll practice and get back on my game,* she decided with a bit of her characteristic determination.

Maggie stashed her groceries and dug into the rotisserie chicken and coleslaw that she bought for her dinner. She began a systematic reconnaissance of the kitchen. To her delight, it was equipped with every specialty pot, pan, and utensil imaginable. *I've been lusting after some of this stuff in catalogs for years,* she thought. *What great fun to cook in this kitchen.*

Along one wall was an enormous antique hutch. Maggie found it contained five complete sets of china, including specialty pieces like eggcups, double-handled soup bowls, and tureens. She recognized Colombia Enamel by Wedgwood and Botanic Garden by Portmeirion, but had to check the bottom of a plate to see that she had place settings for twelve of Derby Panel by Royal Crown Derby and a lovely blue-rimmed favorite called Autumn by Lenox. A set of cheerful yellow Fiestaware completed the collection. *Good Lord*—she felt faint. Maggie was a self-described china addict; now she had the collection to prove it. She vowed to use the good dishes every day.

Maggie made herself tea in a Wedgwood cup and wandered through the house to find a place to tuck herself away to enjoy it. The long day had taken its toll; she was exhausted. As she passed through the archway into the library, she found an overstuffed chair in the moonlight by the French doors and knew she had found her spot. Maggie dragged the sheet off the chair with one hand while waving away a cloud of dust with the other and settled into the chair's protective embrace.

An unblemished blanket of snow in the garden looked like frosting on a cake. At least four inches already, and it was still coming down hard. For the first time in months, everything around Maggie was quiet and still, and she felt peaceful. Thoughts of Paul were always crowding her, and they gradually settled on her now. Who was the man that she had been married to for over twenty-five years?

On the surface, Paul Martin was the charismatic president of Windsor College. Charming and handsome, with a killer smile. And laser focus. When he turned his attention on you, you felt like you were the most inter-esting and important person in the world. She had felt that way for years; had never doubted his integrity or fidelity. Mike and Susan, now both grown and out of the nest, adored their father. Paul's unexpected death at the age of sixty-two had unearthed a number of betrayals. *Were there others yet undiscovered?* He evidently thought he had plenty of time to cover his tracks. Now Maggie was left to cope with it all.

The first shoe to drop was his embezzlement from the college. The interim president discovered suspicious receipts in Paul's desk, receipts that he had been careless enough to leave sitting in a drawer. An audit was hastily done and the results discreetly fed to her. Paul had been submitting fraudulent expenses as far back as they could trace, in excess of two million dollars. Where in the world had he been spending all of this money?

At first, Maggie wondered if Paul had a gambling problem. As she pored through the college's audit, however, it became very clear that the money was being spent in one location: Scottsdale, Arizona. And another fresh hell was born. She would never forget that day, last September, when she had summoned the courage to uncover the identity of the other woman.

Her short flight had been turbulent, and wedged into a middle seat between an overweight man with a dripping nose and a sprawling teenager; she was queasy by the time they landed. Taxiing to the gate seemed interminable. She snatched her carry-on from the seatback in front of her the moment they came to a stop, and shoved past the teen, jostling the woman in the seat across the aisle as she attempted to stand up. "Getting a bit claustrophobic in there," she muttered in a half-hearted apology. The woman huffed and fixed Maggie with an icy stare. She didn't care what anyone thought; she needed to get off of that damn plane. The line in front of her inched along to the door. Why in the hell were people so slow and clumsy with their luggage? Why did they insist on stuffing bags into the overhead bins that they couldn't handle on their own? *Just breathe deeply,* she told herself.

The rental car was waiting for her. Thank goodness for the perks of being a frequent traveler. She settled into the seat and turned the air conditioner on full blast. Maggie fumbled in her purse for the report the private investigator had given her. She double-checked the address, but didn't need to; it was seared into her heart. Maggie punched it into the GPS system, adjusted her mirrors, and began her journey.

It was only ten o'clock in the morning, but near-record temperatures were predicted and heat waves shimmered off the highway. The GPS was reliable, and she was close to the address in under thirty minutes. Maggie decided she needed something to drink and turned into a convenience store to get a giant diet cola and a bottle of cold water. No one was behind her in line, so she took her time fishing out the correct change. Now that she was here, she wasn't so sure she wanted to pick at this scab. She lingered over the rack of tabloid magazines by the door. What was the matter with her? She was just going to drive by a house. She probably wouldn't even see "her." She had come all of this way—she needed to hitch up her britches and do this thing.

Maggie coiled herself into the now oven-like car and burned her hands as she grasped the steering wheel. She took a long pull on her diet cola and set off once more. She drove slowly as the ascending street numbers indicated she was getting close. *Undeniably a swanky neighborhood,* she brooded. *Nicer than ours.* Spacious, new stucco homes with red-tile roofs and soaring arches. Intricate iron gates and ornate light fixtures. Manicured lawns tended by efficient landscapers. No signs of life on this oppressive day. Everyone was safely tucked away.

And there it was. Bigger than the rest—or was she imaging that? It was unquestionably the nicest house on the street. Bile rose in Maggie's throat. If you had lined up photos of all of the houses on that street and asked her which one Paul would have selected, Maggie knew it would have been this house. More grand than their home in California. Maggie drifted across the centerline and caught herself before she hit the other curb. Thank God she was the only car on the street. She needed to get hold of herself; she didn't want to get into an accident right outside the other woman's house. How cliché would that be? She was acting like a stalker, for goodness sake. No one could ever know she had done this.

She turned around in a driveway five houses down

and drove past to view it from the other direction. It looked even better. *That bastard.* She tightened her grip on the steering wheel and turned the car around again, trying to find a shady spot along the curb where she could discreetly watch the house. A couple of palm trees provided the only shade available, and she pulled to the curb. The air conditioning was no match for the midday sun, and she felt like one of the ants that her brother would fry under a magnifying glass on the sidewalk when they were kids. Why in the world had Paul done this? Why hadn't they just divorced? Was he that concerned about the effect it would have on his career? Divorce wasn't a stigma anymore. And he evidently had plenty of money, so splitting what they had in California wouldn't have posed a problem. Surely he knew that she would never have gone digging for more. *Or was he addicted to the thrill of living a secret life?* She instinctively knew she had hit the mark dead center.

Her soda was long gone and she was taking the last swig of water, chiding herself that it was demeaning to be sweltering in a rental car outside of the other woman's house—then she appeared.

Maggie crouched over the dashboard, the air conditioning blasting her hair out of her face, and focused on the other woman like a laser. Tall, thin, and pretty—with shoulder-length blond hair and long, tanned legs—she was laughing with two school-aged children as she herded them into her Escalade. She pulled out of the driveway and glanced in Maggie's direction as she turned to say something to the children in the backseat.

Maggie clutched the steering wheel as nausea overwhelmed her. She tried unsuccessfully to choke it back and grabbed frantically for the empty soda cup and heaved violently. Sweating profusely, she fumbled in her purse for some tissues and a breath mint. The tears she had been holding back for months now broke free. This had been a stupid, crazy thing to do. Why had she expected it to turn out differently? She was a mess. Vomit on her cuff and in her hair. The last thing she wanted to do was spend the day here and get back on a plane later. To hell with the one-way drop-off charge for the rental car. It was only a six-hour drive. She'd be in her driveway about the same time as her scheduled flight was supposed to land. And she wouldn't have to see anyone or talk to anyone along the way. She swung the car around and set her course for home.

The minute she uncovered the Scottsdale connection, Maggie had a gut feeling about what she would find. Paul had supported a second family there. The investigator found that the two children weren't Paul's, thank God. But it had been a long-standing relationship and by the looks of the financial records, he had been supporting her handsomely. The most difficult part of

Maggie's situation was bearing this knowledge alone; she dared not confide in anyone she knew.

Paul had been acting strangely after he took the post at Windsor College eight years ago. And Maggie had done her best to contrive an innocent explanation and rationalize Paul's odd behavior. But everything now made sense: the weekends away, when he was ostensibly too tied up in "strategic planning sessions" to call home; his trendy new wardrobe and haircut; and his younger, more "hip" vocabulary. When Susan pointed this out, Paul laughed and passed them off as his way of relating to the student body.

He had also become increasingly critical of Maggie's blossoming consulting business as a forensic accountant. At first, she believed he was genuinely concerned she was taking on too much and spreading herself too thin. He was emphatic that he needed her by his side for the numerous social engagements required by his position. Somewhere along the way she realized that he resented her success and her growing independence from him. Paul loved to tell his amusing little story about meeting the shy, studious, plain girl in college and turning her into the beautiful, polished, accomplished woman she was now; that their love story was a modern-day *My Fair Lady*. *Ugh!* She might not have been a sophisticate, but she hadn't been a country bumpkin, either. Even Eliza Doolittle outgrew the tutelage of Professor Higgins.

The turning point in their relationship was that horrible fight about the black-tie fundraiser he wanted to chair. He would turn up at the event in his tuxedo and make a nice podium speech, and she would work tirelessly on it for almost a year. She had begged him not to volunteer, told him that she simply didn't have the time, that just this once she needed to focus on herself first. She was about to land a lucrative expert witness engagement she had worked so hard to get. It was a fascinating case and would demand all of her time. And would undoubtedly lead to more such work. She simply could not turn it down.

Paul had railed that he couldn't turn the fundraiser down, either. He started on his usual refrain of "whose job pays more of the bills around here" when Maggie quietly pointed out that her income had exceeded his for several years. For the first time in their more than twenty years of marriage, Maggie had put her foot down and told Paul no. Paul had exploded and they had gone to bed angry. This time, however, Maggie didn't give in or apologize just to keep the peace.

They didn't speak for a week. When they tentatively resumed communication, Paul was derisive and demeaning, constantly criticizing Maggie in matters both large and small. But his opinion of her appearance, her job, and her social skills didn't matter much to her anymore. Maggie's friend Helen summed it up nicely: Paul had lost control of Maggie and he didn't like it. She had half-heartedly defended Paul, saying he was a leader and not a control freak, but she knew Helen was right.

Her lawyer negotiated a settlement of the college's claim against Paul's estate in exchange for his million-dollar life insurance policy. The board of regents hadn't been anxious to have their lax oversight of the college's finances exposed, and Maggie didn't want Mike and Susan hurt by a public discrediting of Paul's memory. She needed to get to the bottom of the mystery that was Paul Martin before she brought Mike and Susan into this nightmare. Maggie hired a private investigator that quickly uncovered the truth.

Revisiting these horribly hurtful revelations—so frustrating because Paul was not there to question, cross-examine, rage at—was like watching a tornado relentlessly obliterate her lovingly crafted life. The pain, loss, and desolation were constant companions. But tonight, sunk into this massive chair within the perfect stillness, Maggie removed herself from the starring role and felt like she was watching someone else's tragedy. She let her mind go blank and watched the snow slanting down across the trees outside her window. And she surrendered to a deep and dreamless sleep.

***

Having his office above his liquor store had its advantages; Chuck Delgado was well into the bottle of Jameson he grabbed from behind the counter as he waited for Frank Haynes to arrive on this Godforsaken night. Shortly after two in the morning, someone tapped quietly on the back door below. Delgado checked the security camera and buzzed him up.

Haynes firmly climbed the steps into Delgado's lair and found him slumped in his chair just outside the pool of light supplied by the green-shaded lamp on his desk. Haynes scanned the room, allowing his eyes to adjust to the dimness. The rest of the room was in shadow, and Haynes was glad of it. He didn't care to be accosted by Delgado's collection of crude, pornographic trinkets and toys.

Delgado shoved the open bottle and a highball glass in his direction. Haynes firmly declined. He didn't need to get lightheaded now, and God knows when that glass had last been washed. He cast a dubious glance at the two chairs across the desk from Delgado, and moved a stack of newspapers and a hamburger wrapper onto the floor. *At least he's eating at one of my restaurants,* he thought.

They regarded each other intently. Haynes remained silent.

Delgado nursed his drink and Haynes sat, brooding and impassive. Delgado finally sucked in a deep breath and began. "Okay, Frank, here's the thing. We ran into an unexpected situation."

Haynes raised an eyebrow.

"Not with anything here. Operations in Westbury are fine. In Florida. It's hard to keep your finger on things from a distance. I sent Wheeler down to check on things, but the bastard spent all his time with the whores in the condos. I understand a guy's gotta have fun, but he didn't do jack shit down there. Bastard lied to me when he got back. If this all goes down, he deserves to take the fall." Delgado gave a satisfied nod and sank back into his chair.

Haynes leaned rigidly forward, resting his elbows on his knees, and locked Delgado with his glare. He waited until Delgado, hand shaking, set his drink down.

"We aren't going to let this 'all go down,' Charles, now are we? We aren't going to let that happen. We had plenty of cushion built in to survive even the Recession. If you hadn't dipped your hand in the till, we wouldn't be having this unfortunate conversation."

"I had stuff to take care of. Those cops down there are expensive and—"

Haynes slammed a fist on the desk and roared, "Silence! I don't care what situation you got your sorry ass into. You know that you were not to bring your sordid business interests into our arrangement. Those condos were supposed to be legitimate investments, not whore houses or meth labs or whatever other Godforsaken activities you've got going in them."

Delgado held up a hand in a gesture of surrender. "You're right, Frank, I know you are. But stuff happens. I'll get this figured out. I may have buyers for a couple of the condos. And I'm expecting money from another associate next week. Enough to fund the shortfall in the next pension payments. Don't go gettin' yourself into an uproar. We'll get things straightened out. I'm on it," he slurred.

"You've got ten days to get this handled," Haynes growled. "I'm going to watch your every move from here on in. You won't want to disappoint me." His tone sent a wave of fear and dread through Delgado.

Haynes rose slowly, turned on his heel, and walked down the stairs, allowing the echo of his steps to recede before he opened the back door and was swallowed by the night.

Delgado held his breath until he could no longer hear Haynes' car retreating. "That guy is seriously unhinged." He reached for the bottle and didn't bother with a glass.

From *Coming to Rosemont*

ABOUT THE AUTHOR

USA Today Bestselling Author BARBARA HINSKE is an attorney and novelist. She's authored the Guiding Emily Series, the mystery thriller collection "Who's There?", the Paws & Pastries Series, three novellas in The Wishing Tree Series, and the beloved *Rosemont Series*. *Guiding Emily* was made into a Hallmark Channel movie of the same name in 2023 and her novella *The Christmas Club* was made into a Hallmark Channel movie of the same name in 2019.

She is extremely grateful to her readers! She inherited the writing gene from her father who wrote mysteries when he retired and told her a story every night of her childhood. She and her husband share their own Rosemont with two adorable and spoiled dogs. The old house keeps her husband busy with repair projects and her happily decorating, entertaining, and gardening. She also spends a lot of time baking and—as a result—dieting.

ALSO BY BARBARA HINSKE

Available at Amazon in Print, Audio, and for Kindle

The Rosemont Series

Coming to Rosemont

Weaving the Strands

Uncovering Secrets

Drawing Close

Bringing Them Home

Shelving Doubts

Restoring What Was Lost

No Matter How Far

When Dreams There Be

Waves of Grace

Threads of Kindness

Love and Legacy

Novellas

The Night Train

The Christmas Club (adapted

for The Hallmark Channel, 2019)

Paws & Pastries

Sweets & Treats

Snowflakes, Cupcakes & Kittens

Tarts & Turnovers

Pies & Plans

Workout Wishes & Valentine Kisses

Wishes of Home

Wishful Tails

Back in the Pack

Novels in the Guiding Emily Series

Guiding Emily (adapted for The Hallmark Channel, 2023)

The Unexpected Path

Over Every Hurdle

Down the Aisle

From the Heart

Growing the Circle

Novels in the "Who's There?!" Collection

Deadly Parcel

Final Circuit

CONNECT WITH BARBARA HINSKE

Sign up for her newsletter at **BarbaraHinske.com**
   Goodreads.com/BarbaraHinske
   Facebook.com/BHinske
   Instagram/barbarahinskeauthor
   Pinterest.com/BarbaraHinske
   BookBub/Barbara Hinske
   Twitter(X)/Barbara Hinske
   TikTok.com/BarbaraHinske
   Search for **Barbara Hinske on YouTube**
   bhinske@gmail.com

www.ingramcontent.com/pod-product-compliance
Lightning Source LLC
Chambersburg PA
CBHW021126070726
47591CB00014B/1554